Pinky Promise Mommy

By
Donna Huff

TATE PUBLISHING
AND ENTERPRISES, LLC

Published by Tate Publishing & Enterprises, LLC
127 E. Trade Center Terrace | Mustang, Oklahoma 73064 USA
1.888.361.9473 | www.tatepublishing.com

Tate Publishing is committed to excellence in the publishing industry. The company reflects the philosophy established by the founders, based on Psalm 68:11,

"The Lord gave the word and great was the company of those who published it."

Book design copyright © 2014 by Tate Publishing, LLC. All rights reserved.
Cover design by Jeffrey Doblados

Published in the United States of America

ISBN: 978-1-62854-017-8
1. Fiction / Romance / Suspense
14.03.04

CHAPTER 1

I WOKE immediately at the sound of screeching tires and crunching of metal in front of my house. It was so loud that the dogs (*I was dog sitting for m*y boss) were barking and dancing around the room wanting to get out. I jumped out of bed and ran to the window and was horrified. A big truck had hit a little car "at least that what it looked like" It was hard to tell because it was so mangled. There was debris all over the road. I could see what looked like a purse, a shoes some clothing and a doll. The truck was dark colored and big with huge tires and wheels, the accident did some major damage to it too. The car looked like it was on its top --- Oh my God--- I could see an arm laying out the broken window. I ran to the phone and called 911. The dispatcher asked a million questions---how many cars involved, was anyone hurt, exact address, time it happened etc. I was so impatient I wanted to see if they needed help so I told her to get someone here quick.

There wasn't anyone out there yet so I grabbed my robe and headed outside As I got to the car I noticed a lot of blood. I didn't want to get to close. The man in the truck was awake and getting out. He had blood all over him but was walking OK.

This was Tuesday I had so many meetings scheduled today. I thought to myself. I looked around and some of the neighbors had heard the noise and come out to see what had happened. Everyone else was just watching. I had to do something but I didn't know what. My eyes went from the accident to the neighbors as if they would tell me what to do. I saw a lady with graying hair walking her dog who had just done his business as she stooped down to retrieve it. She put it in a bag and kept on walking as if nothing had happened and thought to myself this must be one of my neighbors but I didn't know who she was. I didn't know any of them. I kept to myself and hadn't met anyone. Wow I have been here 4 years and don't know any of my neighbors at all.

I walked over to the car and saw a lot of blood coming from under it. My stomach instantly began to churn. This is where the lady was trapped. I looked at the mangled metal and wondered how this could have happened. It was so crunched. I knew most of the cars made but had no clue what this car was... I glanced over my shoulder and saw the street light was still on. There was like a halo around it from a slight bit of fog. I was chilly as I stood there in my housecoat, shivering.

About that time a guy came up---tugged at my arm which pulled me out of my dilemma, he said. "Hey let me through." I moved over still in a state of shock at what I had seen. It was a neighbor trying to help out. He bent down to look in the car and when he got up he shook his head and said "it's bad, really bad."

All of a sudden I heard sirens coming from all different directions, loud screaming noises to go along with the already screaming noises in my head. My head was pounding. My mind was spinning what should I do---what could I do. I didn't know, so I just stood there.

I looked up at my house it was a large house in a quiet neighborhood tree lined streets so how could something like this happen here? My life is very settled for me ---I don't associate with anyone I keep to myself. I go to work, I go home, and I go to bed I had the same routine every day. I have done the same thing for years.

I looked at the car again and tried so hard to figure out what kind it was but it was so mangled there was no way I could figure it out. It seemed like hours before the paramedic and firemen got there but I know it was only a matter of minutes. The paramedics were rushing around the car trying to figure a way to get the people out of it. One guy grabbed my arm and said "hey lady, can you move so we can get in here." "Oh I'm sorry." I overheard them saying there was some kids and a lady in the car as far as they could tell. The man in the truck was going to be OK. He had some cuts and bruises but he would be fine. I headed back inside to get dressed and start some coffee but as I was putting the pot on I glanced out the window and saw the fireman and paramedics rushing around. I headed back outside to see if I could help.

Then I heard this awful noise, it was a fireman very rugged looking with a worried look on his face. He was cutting with the Jaws of Life. He was talking to himself saying "come on cut dam it, cut." The metal was so mangled the Jaws of Life couldn't get a good cut area. "Come on, cut," he kept saying then cursing quietly to his self. The Jaws of Life was jumping around and it was all he could do to hold it. He looked over at me and said "please --- can you bend down there and cover the peoples head and talk to them? Tell them everything will be OK--- were getting them out now. Just reassure them, the kids have got to be scared to death. I'll get this thing going here in a minute."

I leaned down and ask the mother her name she said "Sandy Jenson." I said. "Hi, I'm Amy I need to cover your head so the firemen can cut." --- I told her she would be OK they were working as fast as they could and would have them out shortly. The blanket I was given was too large so someone handed me a jacket to cove her head with.

She looked up at me and said "I know I'm not going to make it, so I want you to do something for me." "Yes you are" I said. "Don't say that." The firemen are going to get you out." She had tears running down her cheeks and smiled just a little smile. Her face must have been pretty but now it was covered with large gashes and blood coming out of her mouth. She looked me straight in the eye and said. "Look I'm a nurse I know how bad I am. But please look after my kids. (She started choking and had to take a minute to finish) I don't have anyone left to take care of them. They need a good home, their good kids and they will be so alone when I'm gone. Please tell me you will help."

I ask her what about family. "Can I call someone for you? I'm sure they would want to know. What's your husband's number. I'll get the phone and call him now." She said no I don't have anyone left. She told me there had been a fire in her house on Christmas Eve 2 years ago. Her Mom & Dad was there from Ohio for the holidays--- they had sang Christmas carols and had a big Christmas dinner before all of them went to bed. Somewhere around 2:00 AM an electrical fire had broken out---her husband had gotten her and their two kids Jason 3 and Shelly 8 out of the house. They were on the bottom floor. Then he went back in after her mom and dad. They had been upstairs sleeping. "As I watched my husband while coughing and choking go back into the house I heard a crash just after he entered, the roof collapse and they were all killed." She said sobbing out of control. I could see it still hurt her very badly. "We were so lucky he got us out alive." She then told me the fire alarms failed to work because she had forgotten to replace the batteries. It was all her fault and now she was going to be with her husband but wanted me to take care of the kids. She especially didn't want them to be in foster homes where they would be split up. I didn't know what to say.

I looked at her and wondered how anyone could ask this of someone they didn't even know. Then I thought she had to be awful desperate to ask a complete stranger to take care of her kids.

CHAPTER 2

HOW COULD I take care of two kids? I didn't know the first thing about kids. I had not been around kids since I was a kid myself. Even then I was a loner and didn't have any friends. I stayed in my room---read or did puzzles. Now at 32 I didn't have a clue what to do. I decided I would tell her OK, I would take them and raise them but all along I knew I wouldn't. It would make her feel better.

My life was set now and I had no room to take care of kids. I didn't want kids. I didn't want the noise or clean up after kids, especially someone else's kids.

I looked back in the rubble of their car and saw a little girl crying and reaching for her mother, this ripped at my heart as she was saying almost in a whisper "Mommy, Mommy, please don't leave me like Daddy did." Her voice was cracking and she sobbed uncontrollably. "Shelly honey it's going to be OK. When we get out of here --- talk to this nice lady she will help you, I love you Shelly take care of your little brother he's going to need you. I love you Shelly, don't ever forget that. Tell Jason I love him too. I will be with you always "

Shelly had blood coming out of her mouth and the large gash on her forehead was bleeding like crazy. I looked up at the fireman - --"how much longer?" He looked at me with eyes that told me it wasn't going very good. I could see the sweat was beading up on his forehead "A little while longer lady, I'm going as fast as I can but the metal is so mangled together it'll take a while longer I'm sorry I'm going as fast as I can." he started cutting again. You could see the determination in his eyes like he knew he didn't have long and needed to get them out now. The noise was so loud my splitting headache was fast becoming a migraine.

I was holding Sandy's hand and it was so cold. I couldn't believe how cold it was. She kept saying please take care of my babies. They need someone they can trust. Jason doesn't remember what happened with the fire --- Shelly is still having a hard time she was so close to her daddy. They played every day and Daddy used to have tea with her. He would sit in her little chair telling me one day he was going to break it. He knew he was too big for it but Shelly insisted he sat with her at the table like big people. She hasn't gotten over him yet --- I'm not sure she ever will. She prays for him and cries herself to sleep every night saying daddy, daddy come back I'll be good I won't ever be bad again. I'll pick up my clothes, brush my teeth. I will be good Daddy just please come home.

I felt my face wet --- I was crying too. This tough exterior that I had spent years building up was crumbling right in front of me. I had made myself into a cold non-caring, unreasoning, non-responsive person who wanted to be alone and work all the time. I had no time for holidays, reunions, picnics, or anything else. This way I wouldn't hurt at the loss of family members. I had loss my family at a young age and didn't want another. I didn't want to go through the pain again. Seeing my mother and father at the funeral home was just too much. I had cut myself off from the world. I didn't have any brothers or sisters and all of a sudden I was alone and lonely. Mom and Dad had been on vacation in China when an earthquake of 7.1 hit then a tsunami. They were both swept away and not found until it was too late. I was still in school so they had my nanny taking care of me while they were gone. I remember Nanny Janie telling me they were both dead. She wasn't very soft, kind of loud and uncaring. I was so hurt. I cried myself to sleep every night too for the longest time.

Oh ya, I had a good income as an executive of one of the largest clothing firms in the Pacific Northwest. I had been in Oregon for the past 12 years and I really liked it there. I did a lot of traveling to buy clothing lines when I first move over here from South Dakota at the young age of 20. I worked my way up to the highest position in the firm. I have traveled all over the world. I drive new Mercedes, I have a nice nest egg in the bank, and I have a big new house, in an exclusive neighborhood. BUT, that was all. These were all material things I could change them every year. I couldn't, no I wouldn't be hurt again. I didn't want a relationship. I wouldn't allow myself to get close to anyone.

My job kept me in town now in a very nice office in a high rise building. I did miss the traveling but I was settled here now. I didn't go to lunch or shopping with the girls. I never attended a company party. I just kept to myself. I did my job and I did it well. My promotions over the years showed that.

My life was passing before me at that time. I looked down at Sandy again and she was closing her eyes. "Hey there don't go to sleep we need you awake. The firemen are going to get you out in just a minute so you need to stay awake." She squeezed my hand and looked up at me and whispered. "I'm losing it, please-please tell me you will take care of my babies." I told her ---"you don't even know me."

"I do know you are a very caring person

to sit here and hold my hand, and keep me talking, --- I can tell because I see love and compassion in your eyes."

"Please tell me you will help my babies." "OK -- OK, hush now don't talk anymore." I told her."look you're going to be OK I will take care of both of your kids until you get better." She kept saying "I'm not going to make it. Please take care of them."
"I will, I will, I promise." She squeezed my hand as hard as she could and said in a hoarse cracking whisper it has to be a *'Pinky Promise.'* "What" I said. She whispered again saying "I want a *'Pinky Promise'* from you." She held her pinky up for me to squeeze. I thought this is crazy I'd never seen anyone do this before ---I put my pinky in hers and said.
"Yes, yes

'Pinky Promise'
She looked up at me and said, "Thank you so much Amy."

CHAPTER 3

I LOOKED UP at the fireman and he knew what I was going to ask. "It looks like it won't be much longer now" he smiled at me and said "You are doing a great job. Hang in there just a little longer. You have been great the way you comforted her." He was looking at me kind of funny.

I didn't realize until the little girls hand started moving that I had been holding her hand all along. She was looking at me wanting to know about her mommy. "They almost have it ready to take you out are you ready?" She shook her head with big tears still running down her cheeks. "Where do you hurt sweetie?"

"My legs hurt so bad she replied and my head."

"OK lay still it won't be long now." They had been in there so long. I had to stop talking my voice was cracking ---I didn't know where Jason was. I couldn't see in the car for all the metal. I hope he was OK. Dear God please let him be ok. Sandy had said he was 3 years old.

"Lady, can you get back were about to take this piece out." the fireman said with a caring shaky voice. "Thank god." I said as I told Sandy they were getting her out now. She had her eyes closed --- I thought to myself she wasn't very old to have so much tragedy happen to her in her short lifetime. Then there was Shelly and Jason what pain they have been through. They lost their Father and both Grandparents at the same time. This was exactly why I wouldn't let myself get close to anyone. The thought of going through that pain again was not a plan in my life.

The fireman was pulling and tugging at

the metal and he turned to me and said "you may not want to see what we uncover when we take this piece off." "Maybe you should stand over there." I think it's going to be bad.

"Ok" I said as I edged my way backwards, --- watching the fireman pulling at the metal. I really didn't want to see what they uncovered, but I knew I couldn't just leave. Some force was keeping me there. I was so engrossed with watching them do their job that as I backed up I stumbled over the curb and landed on my rear end in the grass.

Just then there was another horrifying screech and a loud crash as a dump truck rammed into the already terrible crash site. I looked up and everything was moving down the road (almost in slow motion) being pushed by this huge yellow dump truck. The fireman all scrambled to get out of the way. There were two firemen who were caught up in the crash and had to be pulled out from between the cars, and taken to the hospital. I heard the firemen talking about the guy driving had a heart attack and couldn't stop. They got the driver out of the truck and sent him to the hospital after working on him for 10 minutes or so. They said he was in danger but thought he would make it.

The rest of the firemen continued work on Sandy and her kids, I didn't know what the movement of the extra impact had done to her and the kids but it didn't look good. The car had been moved about 20 feet and off to the side, it was part way upon the curb now. If the fireman hadn't asked me to leave I would have been crushed. I found out later it was a good thing the truck had moved the car because Jason had been trapped and it would have been a lot longer to get him out. When the dump truck hit the car it had freed him from where he was pinned. He was moaning in pain but by this time but he was finally free. Now they can work on getting him out.

As they continued to pull at the metal from the other side of the car I heard a loud scream, it must have come from Sandy. They told me later that her whole body had been tangled up in the metal. When they pulled the car apart it tore her up so bad she wouldn't have had a chance.

She was right and she knew all along she wasn't going to make it.

I overheard the coroner say she had died

instantly. I said "no she didn't I was talking to her the whole time they were cutting her out." They said her neck was slit clear through and she could not have survived---*death was instant.* The coroner said her body temperature told them she had been dead since the accident happened well over 2 hours ago. No they couldn't be right. What did they know ---I was the one talking to her---holding her hand, promising to take care of her kids. Wasn't I?

The coroner had on white jacket and pants with dark rimmed glasses that he was constantly pushing back up on his nose where they belonged. I thought why doesn't he just get glasses that fit right. His hair was a salt n pepper color and very unruly, as a matter of fact it was just a mess. He very roughly put her body on a gurney covered her up then pushed her over by his vehicle. I ask him to put her in the van because the kids may see her. He replied with. "We put all of the dead in the van at once lady." My God I thought how cold he was to not care that these little kids will see their dead mother. I was getting pretty mad and told him "*make an exception---you better put her in the van now or I would.*" He gave me a stern look but started to load her gurney.

Poor little Shelly had a very large gash on her line of her forehead that would take extensive plastic surgery and time to fix. Her leg was so mangled in the wreck and she would probably walk with a limp for the rest of her life. They both would be in the hospital for a while.

They got Shelly out first --- she looked over at the gurney just before the coroner (after taking his sweet time) was about to load her and said crying. "You're going to be with Daddy now, he will take care of you Mommy I love you. I will talk to you every night in my prayers just like I do with Daddy. I will take care of Jason and never leave him." *By this time she was yelling.* "I'll make sure he takes a bath --- eats his food ---goes to bed early just like you did. I will take good care of him. *Pinky Promise Mommy---Pinky Promise.*"

CHAPTER 4

I KNEW I should go see them at the hospital--- I was scared they would want to come home with me. I hadn't slept well since the accident 3 days ago--- I didn't know how to deal with that. I usually sleep like a log. I looked in the mirror as I was getting ready for work ---I looked tired --- my eyes had dark circle under them, "Man I looked terrible" I moaned. Then with a stern look on my face I said out loud "Amy I'm ashamed of you need someone as much as those kids need you. Why are you so afraid to love?" *Look if I wanted someone I would have someone but I don't so get off my back.* This is not good I was talking to myself ---worse yet I was answering myself. I then gave myself a look of disgust and finished getting ready for work. I was trying desperately to not look in the mirror and put it all out of my mind.

I had so many meetings that week I didn't think I would ever get done. I was in the meeting room one day with all of the heads of the company and we were discussing my going to Europe again to buy a line of cloths put out by a new designer. She was a fabulous designer and I was excited to be going. I hadn't been on a trip in a long time and after the accident I was ready. I had been looking over the line of clothing and was explaining what I was intending to purchase when someone put their hand on my shoulder. I thought I had said something wrong and was about to be corrected but as I turned around there was no one there. Wow that was strange. I know I felt a hand. I went on and got through the budget and we all left for the day. The next day something else happened that was strange.

I got in my car and my radio was programmed on the news so I changed the channel which I never do and heard a good sounding song. To my surprise it was a country song. It had good beat so I left it on. I wasn't familiar with the singers because I always listened to the news. I found myself listening to the words. He was singing about a little boy who 'wanted to grow up to be just like his Dad.' It was a catchy song--- Ya I liked it.

As I was listening to the music ---driving to work, I found myself on the street to the hospital. It was in the opposite direction from my office. I have no clue how I got there.

In front of the hospital building there was an ambulance and a fire truck. The man who was standing next to the fire truck looked right at me as I drove past. He looked so familiar. OK, yes it was the fireman who had cut Sandy and the kids out of the car with the Jaws of Life. He was very handsome standing there in the sunlight but that's as far as it went. His eyes followed me as I turned into the parking lot. I sure didn't want him to see me watching him.

When I found a spot to park I got out of the car still not knowing what had brought me here --- "Hey there, aren't you the nice lady that was at the crash site on Melrose Street a couple of days ago? Are you here to see the kids? I'm sure they would love to see you." He said.

"Yes that was me." I answered quietly.

"Look I know this sounds crazy ---I don't know what I'm doing here. I was headed to work this morning and found myself here instead." I said mumbling not really wanting him to hear me. I looked up at the letter A on the sign to see where I had parked. I could remember that Lot A for Amy.

He added as I was turning back. "I've been here quite a bit. I stop in every time I come in with an ambulance. The little boy Jason is pretty banged up with a lot of broken bones, some cuts and bruises. He has both legs in cast and one arm. They said if the dump truck hadn't hit he would have been tougher to get out. Shelly, the daughter I don't know about she has more problems than her injuries-- -she keeps looking out the window saying '*Pinky Promise Mommy-Pinky Promise.*' She doesn't eat so they have had to feed her intravenously. She cries at night and stares out the window during the day. Do you know what she means when she say's *Pinky Promise Mommy*?" I just looked at him and looked away.

I knew exactly what she meant. Her Mom had me do a *'Pinky Promise.'* I had forgotten about that. Great---the tears were there in my eyes again. I didn't want this guy to see me crying. I didn't want anyone to see me cry so I turned away and gave a fake cough and quickly wiped my wet eyes.

"Those poor kids are really going to have it tough." He said with a frown. "Jason keeps asking for his Mommy. They are both up in the pediatric ward. The Dr. put them in the same room. He thought it would help. I'll walk up there with you if you want me to. I have to stay here for a few minutes anyway. They don't have my supplies ready yet."

"Oh you don't have to." I answered as I pushed the key button and locked my car ---I looked around to get my directions and started walking slowly across the parking lot. "I'm sure I can find it just fine. Thanks anyway."

"Nice talking to you. By the way I'm Sammy what's your name?" He yelled as I was leaving.

"Amy, thanks I have to go now."

"Ya, nice talking to you and I'm sure you can find it --- but you're going the wrong way."

He said with a cocky smile on his face. As I

As I flushed I could feel my face turn red I turned and headed the way he pointed ---he went the other way saying. "See ya later". as I watched him leave.

When I got to the pediatric ward I went to the nurse's station and on the counter was a file that said '3/2/02' JENSON, SHELLY. I couldn't put my finger on what it was about that date until later.

"Can I help you miss?" ask a tall lanky nurse with graying hair all pulled back in a bun. I didn't think anyone wore a bun these days. She had a starched white uniform on that fit her thin body like a glove. Straight down no figure at all. Her arms were full of charts that she was about to drop. She quickly put them on the counter and asked if she could help me again. I ask her what room Shelly & Jason were in--- she told me room 32 then she gave me directions ---straight down the corridor to the end turn left 5th door on the right.

CHAPTER 5

AS I WALKED down the hall Dr's and nurses were busy rushing into a room, then I heard 'CODE BLUE'. I leaned up against the wall to get out of the way. They were running ---pushing equipment as fast as they could. They disappeared into the room. It was pretty noisy yelling to get this and that. Then as I continued down the long hallway it was quit with no one around at all. I saw the 5th door with the numbers '32' on the door. I hesitated outside. What am I doing here? I ask myself. I really didn't know. I keep telling myself I just wanted to make sure they were alright. Then I would leave ---go back to my life and forget about this episode that had uprooted my life so much in the past 3 days.

I slowly opened the door, the room was nice and had yellow walls which made it cheery. As I peaked in I saw Jason first. He was in casts on both legs and one arm to his shoulder. He looked so uncomfortable. His one leg was pulled up in the air. I looked up in the corner and saw he was watching cartoons on the TV. He had large brown teddy bear tucked under his arm holding it so tight --- as if he let loose it would go away. He had just eaten and pushed his tray away with his only good arm.

The sheets were done in kids cartoon print and I thought that's cool. It made the kids feel more at home. The walls were painted a bright color of yellow with a light blue trim. I didn't much like the color combination but it was cheerful looking.

Shelly was in the other bed staring out the window. I watched for a couple of minutes and she never moved. As I walked in Jason ask who I was ---I said I was the lady at the crash site who talked to his Mommy. "Where's my

Mommy? They said she was in heaven with my Daddy."

"That's right sweetie she's with Daddy. What are you watching?" I asked.

"A wabbit show, do you see wabbit show?" He said in a 3 year olds voice.

"No, I watch the news, but that sounds like a good show." He looked at me with a confused look and said. "What's newts?"

I had to laugh as I told him it was an adult show about what was going on in the world.

"Oh" he said as he turned back to the TV. He started laughing at the cartoon and got caught up in it so I turned to the other bed with Shelly in it.

I caught a glimpse of Shelly turning a bit in bed saying '*Pinky Promise Mommy-Pinky Promise*' Shelly never took her look away from the window. The nurse came in and tended to Jason. She looked over at me and said.

"He will be in cast for about 6 weeks, it's tough on a little guy of his age. They like to run & play. He broke his legs up pretty bad but they'll heal in time." She looked over at Shelly and said "I don't know about Shelly---she never looks anywhere else but out the window. She keeps saying *Pinky Promise Mommy Pinky Promise.*"

I watched her for a few minutes before I walked over to her bed and sat down next to her. The top part of her head was bandaged up. The nurse had told me she had a very jagged cut from one side of her forehead to the other. They were going to do the first of many surgeries on Friday --- it would take many surgeries to correct the scars, even then they probably won't be able to correct all of them. Her leg needs more surgery so they will work on that in between.

I told the nurse about the fire and her Daddy and grandparents being killed. She was glad I told her because now they know why she just stares out the window. They have had a psychologist coming in to talk to her and this would really help. I could tell the nurse was worried about her by the look on her face. She had what looked like tears in her eyes and was fighting to hold them back. "She's such a beautiful little girl. She reminds me of my own daughter."

"I know it's a shame they have to go through

this and without either parent." I replied.

I looked at her and ask if she remembered me. I told her I was the lady who held her hand and talked to her Mommy. She turned and looked at me for a minute then turned back to the window. I told her I would come back and see her if she wanted me to. She shook her head yes, but still never stopped looking out the window.

I left that day with a heavy heart, not knowing what to do. When I arrived at work everyone was asking where I had been. I was never late to work or never took off work so this was a first. I told everyone to get back to work everything was fine....I did get some strange looks from a couple of girls, but as I shot them a look they knew they needed to get back to work and let it go. I was a pretty hard boss but that's how I got where I am today. I had three very possible employees who I would move up as soon as the time was right.

I went into my office and could see all the busing going on. I tried to concentrate but it was no good. All I could think about was those two darling little kids in not only physical pain, but the pain of loosing their mother as well. *So sad, so sad* I thought.

CHAPTER 6

I FOUND MYSELF not being able to concentrate or do my work all day. I finally left 10 minutes early--- got caught up in rush hour traffic and had a splitting headache. The cars honking and what for there was nowhere anyone could go, but they kept honking, honking, honking. I just wanted to scream 'STOP' It took me 30 minutes longer to get home that day. When I arrived home there was a note on my door. It was from the fireman. He wanted to know if I could stop see Shelly and Jason for the next 3 days or so. He said he had come down with a cold and didn't want o give it to them. He had been there every day and Jason really seemed to like his stopping by. He didn't want everyone to abandon them at once. He wrote his name Sammy Jinson (how weird the kid's mothers name was Sandy Jenson) along with a phone number (555-3202 so I could call and confirm I was going to stop by.

At first I thought boy the nerve of this guy. Then I thought of Jason and Shelly being alone again. I found myself wondering if this guy had kids of his own, was he married, 'Stop it' quit thinking this way it's none of your business besides what do you care.

Lots of things having to do with this accident have been very weird. I found myself saying out loud. The accident happening right in front of my house, the paramedic saying Sandy died instantly, it happened on 3/2/02, (my birthday which I don't celebrate) finding myself at the hospital, the kids were in room 32, (I'm 32) Sandy and Sammy having similar first names and same last names (different spelling) The fireman's phone number 3202. Boy I'm getting paranoid.

I went to the bathroom and ran some hot water, I just wanted to soak for while. I poured the bubbles in and then poured more in. I wanted lots of bubbles so I could just hide in them. Then I put some coffee on while waiting for the bath to fill up. I took some aspirin, lit some candles, --- slid in the tub to take a long hot bath.

The coffee was ready and tasted really good. I needed to finish some work I had brought home from the office. So I laid it all out on the desk when I saw the note from the fireman. I guess I should call him maybe he will be able to get someone else to check on the kids. I really didn't have time.

I started to pick up the phone when the dinger went off on the microwave. My healthy nuked dinner was ready. After putting it on the table along with my napkin, silverware, and glass of milk I then sat down. I remembered the phone call. I went to the phone and dialed the number. A hoarse sounding man answered the phone and I hesitated 'after he said hello.' He then said, "hello" again.

I replied, "This is Amy Grant the lady from the

accident the other day."

"Oh hi, how's it going? Sorry I'm a little under the weather --- picked up a darn cold."

"Um, I just wanted to call you back and see if you could find someone else to stop by the hospital. I'm going to be really busy the next few days and don't think I can make it." "Oh." He said sounding somewhat disappointed. "I'll have to see what I can do but thanks for calling." With that he said goodbye and hung up. As I sat back down to eat I wasn't hungry I looked at the Salisbury steak and gummy potatoes on my plate grabbed it got up and threw it in the trash. By this time it was all cold anyway.

Funny after I told Sammy Jinson I couldn't make it to see the kids I found myself there for the next week. I found myself going by every day. I'm not sure why this guy felt obligated he never said.

Every day was better than the first. Jason was loosening up and laughing a lot. He had the nurses all loving him so much. Yes, I think I was hooked to! Shelly was still staring out the window. I thought this was going to take her a long time to get better. I stopped at the store and brought books, stuffed animals, crayons, candy whatever I though kids would like. Shelly's things hadn't been touched, so I piled them up on her table so when she was ready she could reach them. Jason loved everything I brought and especially the blue elephant he kept it with him and his teddy bear (I found out Sammy had brought him the bear) they were his constant companions. He had one animal under one arm and one animal under the other arm. We talked and laughed and watched *wabbit* cartoons. I found myself loving it.

I was so worried about Shelly. She had her first surgery and everything went well but didn't change her attitude. She was always so sad. Somehow I had to break her shell and get her back to being a kid again. I didn't want to push her, I was afraid she would go deeper in her shell. I had to let her come out when she was ready. I watched her move around in the bed never ending trying to get comfortable. She just was so uneasy and never stopped staring out the window. As if she was talking to someone without uttering a word. The only thing she ever said was *Pinky Promise Mommy-*

Pinky Promise.

CHAPTER 7

AFTER 5 DAYS Sammy came in one morning when I was about to leave. He looked surprised saying.

"I thought you didn't have time to come by. I ask Ester to come by every day."

"I found some time after all." I shot back at him.

"I thought you might that's why I told Ester to not worry about it I was sure you would be here." his comment with that same cocky smile. What ego this guy has how him dare he talk about me to someone I don't even know. Talk about nerve this guy's not for real.

I gathered my expensive Coach purse and custom designed jacket and said goodbye to Jason. He reached up and kissed me on the cheek.

"Amy I wove u come see me." He said. With the cutest smile.

"OK sweetie I'll be back" with that I blew him a kiss and went to say goodbye to Shelly.

I usually sit there a minute and stroke her hair telling her things would get better it would just take time. You need to tell people what you want and what you need. No one knows unless you tell someone. "I'll see you tomorrow." I bent down and kissed her on the nose. I thought for just a second she responded but I guess not.

I left the room and Sammy followed me telling the kids he would be right back. I looked over at Sammy in the hallway ---he had that damn cocky smile on his face again.

"What." I asked.

"Oh nothing I was just thinking for someone who spends all their time in an office, and home, with no social life you sure would make a great mother."

"You don't know anything about me,---I would appreciate if you wouldn't pry into my life. Look my personal life is my business."

"Well excuse me. I remembered what you said you told the kids mother. There was something special there, something going on that even you didn't know about. I thought you were going to take care of the kids. At least you implied you were. You were talking to yourself the whole time you were holding the lady's hand."

I answered him bluntly "I just said that because I thought she wasn't going to make it. It made her feel better in her last couple of hours alive. Knowing her kids would be OK."

"Amy, I think you were meant to be with those two kids." he said softly.

"Look why don't you have dinner with me tonight and I'll tell you what I know about it and why you were meant to be with those kids." After a few minutes of excuses I gave in and agreed to meet him at 7:00 for dinner.

I arrived at the restaurant a little early so I found a spot at the bar. This guy sitting 3-4 seats down from me was staring at me. It was really making me uncomfortable. I ask the bar tender to ask him to stop staring. He came back and said the guy wanted to buy me a drink. I said no I was waiting for someone. That's when the guy wouldn't take no for an answer and came over and sat next to me. He reeked of beer and I could tell he had too much to drink. The bar tender came over and told him to leave me alone and move seats. He said he didn't want to he was happy right where he was. Just then he reached over and grabbed my leg. I jumped and the bar tender was around the bar fast. The guy got lucky a punch in and the bar tender went down to the floor. The guy grabbed me and said let's get out of here. I tried to jerk away but he was a big guy and I couldn't get away. Next thing I knew he had a knife at my throat.

I started to scream but he held the knife closer I could feel the cold blade against my skin. It was stinging. I knew all he has to do is make one move and I would have a slit throat. My mind was racing what should I do now. Oh my God I thought what is happening am I going to die? These past few days have been horrible. I couldn't think, the drunk was staggering and I just knew he was going to cut me.

Sammy came in about that time and was

shocked at what he saw. I was never so glad to
see someone in my life. The guy started
pushing me out the door with him. As he
approached Sammy he said
"Don't try to stop me dude I'll cut her. I
really will."
"Hey don't worry, I don't even know her I
could care less." Sammy shot back laughing.
"Smart guy now get out of the way."
"I was just about to have a drink would you join
me."
"Hey mate sounds good but first I have to take
this little lady out to my truck and show
her what a real man is." He grabbed at my arm
and squeezed tight. I twisted my arm and
tried to wiggle out of his grip. While looking at
Sammy to do something.
Sammy pulled his hand loose and said "I wish
you wouldn't do that she doesn't look worth it."
He looked over and winked at me then turned
back to the drunk and continued.
        "Hey I know where we can get some
women that will do just about anything we
want." The drunk stumbled, a little as he said
"Sounds good, how far away is it?"
        Sammy looked over at the door and said

"not far at all turn around and look." As he went to turn Sammy grabbed the knife and knocked him to the ground. The police were right there to handcuff him and haul him to jail. Someone had called the police when this all started. The drunk was arrested and we went to the other side to have dinner.

As we sat down I was still shaking, I told Sammy "I don't know whether to thank you or be insulted."

"Hey," he responded "sometimes you have to say what comes to mind first. Kind a like what you did huh."

"Look, I just said what that lady wanted to hear."

He reached over and took my hand in his and said. "Amy, I checked the ladies pulse when we got there --- wrist and neck, believe me she was dead already. All of the time you were talking to her she was gone. She wasn't talking back. She was already gone….. You say she was talking to you---no one heard her but you. Why do you think her hand was so cold." he insisted. "That's why I say you were meant to be with Shelly & Jason." "No, she made me do a Pinky Promise with her she gave me her pinky to squeeze." I answered with my voice trembling. I was so confused I knew what I heard and saw. It was real I know it was. I can't explain it otherwise.

CHAPTER 8

"MY LIFE HAS been so messed up for the last week I don't know what to do." I choked out in between sobs. I didn't realize the tears were flowing and Sammy had moved over next to me and was comforting me. I cried for a while with my head on his shoulder and he just let me. He kept saying everything would work out ok. Everything was a blur, what did all of this mean? After I calmed down we talked for what seemed like hours. I still refused to believe the lady wasn't alive. I talked to her. Now trying to figure out what all of this meant and what to do.

"Look why don't you talk to someone it's pretty apparent you have some issues with all of this." Sammy quietly said.

I went home completely drained and called into work sick the next day. I needed to think and make a decision. I needed to see Shelly & Jason, I needed to talk to them. I headed to the hospital stopping along the way at the toy store to get a couple of books for them. I had a large house 4 bedrooms plenty of room. I just didn't know how to take care of them. I was scared--- what if I screwed up. What if they got sick and I didn't know what to do. What do I cook for them I eat microwave stuff all the time. I really don't know how to cook.

When I arrived at the hospital it was almost as a weight had been lifted from my shoulders. Sammy was in the room when I got there. I ask him to join me in the hall for a minute.

"Sammy, I don't cook, what if their sick, what about school I don't know the first thing, what if Shelly gets a boyfriend, what if Jason gets in a fight."

"Whoa hold on, your going too fast, what are

you talking about?"

In a determined voice I replied "I'm taking the kids to live with me, I'm going to adopt them. What do you think? That's what I'm supposed to do isn't it? (I was looking for a answer from Sammy.) It came to me this morning. All this time I was supposed to take Sandy's children and raise them. I do have a big house and good job and money in the bank. I don't know why she talked to me that day, she really must have seen how unhappy I had been and knew her precious kids would make my life complete."

"Boy." Sammy said, "This is all a lot to take in at one time. Sounds like you have your mind made up." I looked up at him and said.

"Yes I do."

"Ok then I'll help you all I can." He whispered.

"Thanks Sammy I was counting on that. Let's go tell the kids."

At that moment I felt like I had known Sammy all my life. He was a special person. He came in the room with me and I ask Jason if he wanted to come live with me when he got out of the hospital. He started yelling and saying "ya, ya, ya, I gona wiv wiv Amy." He looked over at Shelly and said in a quiet voice "Shedy," goin wiv wiv Amy too?" (He didn't have all of his words down yet we would have to work on it.) I looked at Sammy and he was all smiles. "Yes Jason, I said Shelly too." He gave me a big smile and big thumbs up.

Shelly said nothing so I went over and sat down beside her and ask her if she wanted to live with me. She was still staring out the window. She didn't say anything. "You know, that's what you're Mommy wanted you and Jason to do." I told her as softly as possible. I sure didn't want to upset her. Then I added. "I don't want to force you to do something you don't want to do. So you think about it for the next day or so and let me know. You will both be getting out of here in about 4 days. I won't be replacing your Mommy she will always be your Mommy. I would just be taking care of you."

I looked over at Sammy--- the smile was gone and he had a look of concern. We knew there was a problem still with her. She just couldn't accept her mommy being gone too. What would she do if she refused to go home with me? That bothered me a lot. I looked at her again hoping to get some kind of reaction but nothing. I started to get up and bent down and kissed her on the nose again. I rose and started to turn when I felt something on my arm. Oh my God it was Shelly reaching for me, tugging on my sleeve. I sat down again---she grabbed me and hugged me like she wouldn't let go. I hugged her back. She finally spoke and said. "I was waiting for you to say you wanted us to live with you. You did a Pinky Promise with my Mommy."(did Shelly really hear us do the Pinky Promise?) "I love you Amy. I want to go with you and Jason and Sammy. You can be our new Mommy and Daddy……. I'm going to be so ugly no one will love me but you and Daddy." My heart skipped a beat. Oh great, what do I do now she thinks Sammy is going to be her Daddy. I looked over at Sammy and he had a look of happiness on his face. I don't think he had heard what she said.

We said our goodbyes and told the kids we would see them in the morning. When we got in the hall I told Sammy we needed to talk tonight. "OK, I'll come over to your place and we can look at the bedrooms and see if you want to change them." Sammy said with a still light air to his voice.

"Ok see ya at 7:00" I said.

Sammy stopped to tell the nurses Shelly was talking. He wanted to make sure they knew so if she wanted anything they would be there for her. They were excited and a couple of them ran into her room to talk to her. As I started walking down the hall I knew I had a lot of thinking to do again. Boy, this thinking was tough. I had to be careful with Shelly she had just come out of her shell. I didn't want to send her back in. She was so vulnerable right now.

When Sammy showed up I was looking at the TV but not seeing what was on. My mind was spinning. I just didn't know if I did the right thing. Sammy came in and we talked for a long time. I finally decided it was for the best to bring them home with me and do my best.

We left the hospital with Shelly still in a daze. As the days wore on she loosened up a bit but still had that empty look to her. My heart was braking seeing this beautiful little girl go through so much pain. I knew I couldn't help her. This was something she had to work out on her own. As the days turned into months and then years we were settled in our routines. The kids got up I got them off to school and then tackled picking up and work at home. I wasn't making as much as before but we were doing ok.

I was learning a great deal about parenting but it wasn't all good. There were defiantly ups and downs along the road. Sammy was great he would take the kids to get ice cream and give me a break. Then one day all hell broke loose. Shelly was in one of her moods and was screaming all day at anyone in her way. "You never wanted me to come live with you." She yelled at me. I had been trying to be nice to her but after her comment I decided to send her to her room. "I don't care I'll stay there for the rest of my life. It's a ugly room and I hate it." She added with tears in her eyes as she ran out of the kitchen.

What had I gotten myself into? Was this going to last forever? I didn't have the answers but I did know one thing. I made a promise "*A Pinky Promise*" and I was going to keep it.

CHAPTER 9

SHELLY WAS GETTING older and I could see she was going to be any boys dream girl, except for her attitude. She really needed to work on that. When Sammy came over off and on to take the kids places Shelly would be as sweet as she could. They went to the park and firehouse, swimming, movies whatever they wanted to do.

Sammy and I spoke but about the kids and weather, we never dated or anything like that. We just associated through the kids. I would tell him about how Shelly was acting and he would tell me it was just in my head, she was a sweet loving little girl. This went on for about 3 years and Sammy was so active. I guess being a fireman he had to keep in shape. I let them go do their thing even though I was invited I always said no thanks maybe another time. I didn't want to interfere with the time they had together. I knew Sammy loved both kids very much.

Shelly had calmed down enormously and was getting on my good side again. She would play with Jason and once in a while help around the house. I really appreciated that and told her so. We were finally getting along good.

I have learned a lot about raising kids and it hasn't been easy but I wouldn't change a thing. I just wish their mom and dad could be here to see how great they have turned out.

Christmas came and went then spring into summer. We were all getting along fine. Jason had been working on his speech and was easier to understand and Shelly was just finishing the 5th grade. Shelly was well developed for her age and taller than most of the girls in her class. She had changed some but I decided it was just a faze she was going through. I had started her in dance and she didn't like it so then she wanted to do gymnastics she didn't like that either. I didn't say much thinking she was just confused and would find something she liked eventually.

Sammy and I were getting a little closer by now and he would stay longer after bringing the kids home. We would have dinner with him cooking. I have to say he was a good cook. We did BBQ a lot and Jason played in the yard and Shelly was usually on her phone texting someone. I couldn't imagine what there was to say that took so long on the phone. I bought her a laptop for the last Christmas and she liked to play games on it. Until I found out by accident she was in chat rooms. One chat room was older guys, well I put a stop to that right away and took her laptop away. She was furious with me but that was something I wasn't going to tolerate. "You just don't want me to have any friends, all we do is talk." She screamed at me.

"Shelly you don't just talk to older men you don't know. There's a lot of perverts out there who are just waiting to hurt little girls." "You just don't get it do you?"she screamed at me. "I'm not a little girl anymore you can't tell me what to do because you aren't my real mother are you?"

I sat there shocked at what she had just said. "No, I'm not your real mother but right now I'm the only mother you have so now you can go to your room until dinner time." I shot back at her. I hated to fight with her but I lose my temper like she does. She shouldn't talk to me that way. Wow what am I doing wrong now? I heard the bedroom door slam shut and ignored it. If I went in there it would just be another fight. My head was busting and I didn't need to get into it again with her. So I folded the cloths that Shelly was suppose to fold and sat down with my book to read and a hot cup of coffee. It smelled so good I wanted to get lost in my book.

The minutes turned in to 2 hours and it was getting time to fix dinner so away went the book. Jason had just come back from the next door neighbors and wanted something to snack on. Out came the apples to tide him over. As I started dinner Jason was staring at me. I asked. "Jason, why are you staring at me?" "I think your pretty like my mommy."

"That's so sweet Jason and yes your mother

was very pretty," with that he looked down and started eating his apple. He then got up and ran from the room.

Dinner went off without a hitch and then baths and bedtime. I slept like a baby that night. I don't know if it was the reading or just plain tired. But it was a good night sleep well needed.

Oh that smell of coffee seemed so much better this morning I have to have another cup. I had been looking out the window remembering the accident that changed my whole world. It had just been a few short years ago and yet I could see it as vivid as if it were happening now. My skin felt funny and I had goose bumps. As I looked out I saw the car overturned and the truck with the man wondering aimlessly along the road. It took me through the years as Amy the career woman to Amy the full time mom. My head started spinning and I had to shake myself out of it. There was no good reason to go over it again. I headed to the kitchen to get another cup of coffee when I felt a tug on my leg it was Jason smiling up at me with those big blue eyes. I swear they were beautiful.wov u." he said shyly. " I love you too sweetie." I smiled back --- picked him up and gave him a big bear hug. He was holding onto me for dear life. When I put him down he said. "I'm so hungry."

"OK, I'll get you some cereal unless you might want pancakes?" He didn't hesitate to say yes. He did love pancakes. He called them 'panycakes'

"Where's sister is she awake?" I ask. "No she till sweeping" he replied. "We'll let her sleep longer and wake her when the pancakes are done Ok." "schur" All of a sudden he ran off saying pee, pee. OK hurry I said as he rounded the corner to the bathroom.

About that time Shelly came dragging in with her eyes half closed bumped into the table and yelled stupid damn table. "Hey there what did you say?"

"Well the table hurt my toe."

"Yes, but you shouldn't be cursing, It's not nice or lady like."

"Well," she said –"I'm not a lady yet so I guess I can cuss if I want to"

"Oh no you can't young lady"

"See" she said, "I'm not nice at all and I can't help it." with big tears in her eyes. I went over and hugged her and told her she just wasn't awake yet, to calm down and I would fix her a pancake. She put her head down and sighed.

CHAPTER 10

WHEN BREAKFAST WAS over Jason went out in the back yard to play on the swing set and I started picking up dishes. When Shelly wandered in she said she wanted to go to the park. I told her maybe later when I was finished picking up the mess. She got mad again and started throwing a fit. She was yelling at me, "get out of my way I'm going to the park." Man, she had so much hostility I didn't know how to handle it. I stood in front of her and told her we would go later and to stop being so childish. That really made her mad.

Just before she ran out the door she stood there and glared at me with a look in her eye I hadn't seen before---like she hated me. She put her hands on my chest and gave a big push and I lost my balance and fell on the end table sideways busting my lip open and hitting my head on the corner. Hurt like hell! I was dazed and slowly got up and went to the bathroom to wipe the blood from my lip. I could feel a warm sensation of blood on my forehead. Oh my word I looked in the mirror and blood was gushing from my head. I put a towel over it and wiped but it wouldn't quit bleeding. By then my head was throbbing I could feel like needles prickling in my head. I knew I had to go to the ER and probably have stitches.

Shelly was in so much trouble. I was going to ground her for the rest of her life.

What do I do about Shelly--- she had left for the park? I guess I'll have to call Sammy. I'm sure he will come over if he isn't working. I found the phone and dialed 555-1234. I was barely able to see the numbers. When he answered I told him what had happened he said he would be right over. It was just what seemed like seconds when he knocked on the door. I had been bleeding so much I was getting light headed. I told him about Shelly leaving and going to the park. Jason was at the neighbors and Jason's friend Kevin and him were playing so Kevin's mother said she would watch Jason. Sammy said. "I'm getting you to the ER first them I'll come back and find *little miss prissy.*" He drove faster than I think he should have and when we arrived it seemed like they were waiting for me. He helped me in and told the nurse what had happened. I could tell he was mad--- I told him, "Don't be too hard on her." He didn't say anything at first then he said. "Don't worry I'll take care of it." They took me into a room and just before I got to the gurney the lights went out. I don't remember anything else until I woke up later in a hospital room with the worst headache I had ever had.

I heard a familiar sound coming from outside the room. As I looked for the call button I noticed a nurse coming into the room.

"Well your finally awake, how do you feel?"

"I've been better." I replied. "Where's Jason he's a little boy--," she stopped me short and said. "I know-- he's just outside playing with the nurses. You're neighbor said he was so worried she had to bring him down here to see you were ok. He is so funny and very worried about you."

"Is Sammy here?" "No, he said to tell you he would find Shelly and bring her back." He planned on having a long talk with her to straighten her out. I'm sure he won't be long.

But he didn't come for the longest time. I have been waiting and Jason was sitting on my bed watching his favorite cartoon Sponge Bob. He sat so quietly -- then all of a sudden he would burst out in laughter rolling around on the bed like a nut. "*Cwazy ponge bob*" he would say.

By this time it was getting dark and I was starting to worry about Shelly --- had Sammy found her? Had she been kidnapped? Had she been hurt? All kinds of thoughts were going through my mind. Sammy had to find her safe --- he just had to.

The medicine must have made me dose off because the next thing I knew was Sammy was holding my hand and said. "If I would have known you were going to pass out on us I would have stayed and tickled you to keep you awake. You missed all the action of having what they said something like 33 stitches and a concussion to go with them…..Boy you got really bad gash on your head. They did some plastic surgery on it. I guess it was pretty torn up."

"Shut up please, did you find Shelly?"

"Not for a while, I drove all over -- walked the park 5 times, Jason mentioned tunnel and then I remembered she like to hide in the tunnel when she was younger. I almost gave up then I saw her. She was all huddled up in the far corner sitting in the water and mud. I took her home first so she could clean up. You know ---she's gotten older---she has some issues --- I don't think you or I can help her with."

"I know that now after the way she acted today. I'm going to try to get her with a therapist. Maybe she'll talk out her anger. I thought she was doing good --- then all of a sudden she started rebelling and acting out, yelling, screaming, now this. I just don't know how to get to her. I started to choke up and Sammy said hush don't worry about it now"

"I know she's hurting and I don't want to

make it worse." I added. My mind started wondering---was she doing drugs, I know she is young but kids have started at her age and younger, would she get worse, I don't know if I would be able to cope with her.

I was let out of the hospital 2 day later. Sammy had taken time off and took the kids to his house. He was great with them. I don't know what I would do if he wasn't there for us. If Shelly was giving him a hard time he never mentioned it. I knew it was going to be hard raising Jason and Shelly but I didn't expect it to be this hard. My biggest concern was Shelly acting up with him. With the kids getting older they were changing so much. Jason always wanted to be the helper and Shelly having a real attitude.

I have had them now for 3 years and Jason doesn't seem to have grown up much. He is in speech classes because he talks with a lisp. The kids at school make fun of him but he takes it all in stride. He just ignores them. I keep telling him he'll get over it.

CHAPTER 11

SHELLY ON THE other hand has let her emotions take over and she rebels against everything. She seems to hate the world and everyone in it. I have tried but don't know how to get through to her. She's not a teen yet but too old to be a little girl, ½ way in-between is not good. At first she was so polite and sweet--- a very loving child. Then -- like overnight something change her completely. Her grades started to go down the attitude started, I don't for the life of me know what went wrong…This is something I hope a therapist can work out with her.

I had not seen Shelly since I fell. She hadn't come to see me in the hospital or called to apologies yet. She seemed to be in a shell, so I thought I'd let her be, and in her own time she would talk to me. After all I wasn't the one who had started this thing.

Sammy thought it better for him and the kids to come home and watch over me. I have to admit it was nice having someone care. He made dinner and got the kids ready for bed that night. For that I was appreciative I didn't want to deal with anything but getting rid of this horrible headache. Sammy had been in and out of my life in the last 3 years, he was working a lot but he did stop by occasionally to see the kids. He would stay around an hour or two at a time, sometimes for dinner.

It felt like the top of my head was going to explode. The pain pills the hospital had given me just didn't work. The Dr. said I would probably have a nasty scar. He gave me a card from a plastic surgeon. I figure I'll wait and see what it looks like.

"Hey there" Sammy said, "how's the patient?" "Can I get you anything?"

"No thanks" I replied "I'm fine just
sleepy---probably the pills"
"Ok" he said as his phone started ringing.
He walked off to answer it.
"I need to leave will you be all right?"
"I'll be OK, what's up" I ask as he had
a troubled look on his face and was
fumbling with his phone,
"Well you'll hear about it soon enough---
there's been a shooting at the mall. From
what they know there were 20-30 people
shot and some are dead. A gunman just
went wild shooting everyone in his sight, I
have to go help".
 "Go, go!" I said "go help and keep me
informed. My God what is wrong with people?"
      "I'll check on you later---he put his hand
on my shoulder, leaned down and said. "The
kids are asleep if you need anything call me,
ok?"
"Ok, just go!" For a minute I thought he
was going to kiss me. When he left I was so
sad why do people do these things? I turned
over and decided to get some rest. I couldn't
sleep--- just toss and turn. Wondering
what was happening at the mall. I turned the

TV back on and was watching but not seeing it. My heart was aching for those people. Earlier I had heard sirens, lots of them. I couldn't imagine the panic at the mall.

I watch the news but I don't like seeing all the violence it's scary. Now with the mall shooting I won't want to go there for a while. Shelly liked to go there with her friends on weekends but it looks like that won't happen either. She'll just have to get mad at me. I can't let her go when I can't be there to protect her. I knew this would start another terrible fight between us. I was going to put my foot down and keep her away for now. Boy I sure got in over my head. I found myself wondering if I had done the right thing by taking them in.

Lately she had been so withdrawn and crabby. I tried to talk to her several times but she just got up and left the room. I was having a hard time coping with her. The school called several times to say she wasn't doing her work in school and her grades were dropping fast. I had heard maybe drugs were the problem but I hadn't seen any drugs around and I just figured it was because of all the bad things that had happened to her. She was getting older and remembering the past. I tried to pass it off as growing up pains but I couldn't do that any longer. I knew she had a problem.

"Well I'll talk to her when we are talking again" I said out load so I could hear myself and think I was in charge. Ya, right ' I was in charge' that's a joke.

CHAPTER 12

A FEW YEARS AGO I wouldn't have thought a thing of the mall shooting. I was always too busy ---I was so hard and callus. I didn't care what was going on in the world. All I cared about was my image, my job, my money, my car, myself….. When I look back at the person I was I think to myself. '*What a witch I was.*' I have changed so much and it was the kids who made me change and Sammy.

My life was so cold and lonely back then. Work, home, traveling that's all I cared about. I didn't have time for anything else. I can't believe how my life had changed. I did miss the excitement of the fashion shows and the travel was great. I had been all over the country.

It's kind of like my friend who was just the opposite of what I was. She would go with a guy just if he had money. She meet this guy whose parents were doing OK--- had a nice big house, lots of cars; they had race cars---show cars. She thought she could get something from the parents through their son, but it turned out they saw right through her and hated her from the beginning because she was ruining their son's life. They found out later she ruined everything she touched. I knew she was wrong but I didn't care that was her problem. I finally lost touch when I found out she had gone crazy and was institutionalized. She was an evil and conniving person through and through. I guess as I look back she had it coming. All of the people she brought pain to would rest in peace.

My mind went back to the kids. My greatest fear today is losing Jason and Shelly. I made a promise and I intend to keep it. They have been life changing to me, for the better I might add.

I heard a car in the drive and half sat up

with head still throbbing. The door opened and it was Sammy. His head was hung and eyes red and swollen. I could see black on his face from the fire that a gunman had started. He looked terrible.

"Sammy, are you Ok?" I ask him.

"No, I'm not, it was a mess so many hurt and killed." He had a strange look on his face. "I couldn't stay any longer after---- I just wanted to get out of there." (His voice was cracking as he spoke) "I'm numb Amy--- shocked and so hurt. I--I just saw my brother Stan lying on the ground with a bullet in his head. He's dead, he's dead, I couldn't stay it was horrible. He started to cry and I felt so bad I didn't know what to do."

"Oh my God Sammy --- I'm so sorry." I said. I had tears welling up in my eyes as well.

Stan was Sammy's younger brother by 4 years. I had met him about a year ago. He had looked up to Sammy. You could tell Stan admired Sammy. Stan was a quite very shy man with wavy hair and a scruffy beard. He stood about 6'3 and was taller than Sammy's 6'1 height He was a construction worker with a large company that traveled to 3 states doing mostly state jobs. He was taller than Sammy but thinner with a dirty blond hair. Sammy's hair was not real wavy but nice looking. Sammy worked out a lot and was solid built. Sammy said he had to keep in shape---it was pretty demanding work that he did. Using the jaws of life, turning cars over if need be, tracking up and down hills for auto's that had went over the side.

He sat on the edge of the bed and I could see tears in his eyes and running down his cheeks. All I wanted to do at that moment was hold him--- to make the pain I saw in his eyes go away. "I'm so sorry. Can I do anything?" He just shook his head. I grabbed him and held him --- the tears came, he cried and cried. Sammy and his brother were so close I knew he would never get over it. I held him stroking his hair for what seemed like a long time. All of a sudden he jumped and said. "I have to go see my parents I have to tell them." He hesitated a minute then added. " Amy I saw him lying there with a hole in his head. Do you know what that feels like to see your brother?" He trailed off and didn't finish the sentence but I knew he was hurting really bad.

"It's going to tear my parents apart." He looked at me and touched my check with his hand ever so gently. "Thank you so much --- I really appreciate you being here for me. I've got to go --- I'll see you when I get back." With that he leaned over and softly kissed me. I was so surprised it was as if fireworks had gone off all around me. I had never felt like this before when I was kissed.

I had met his parents only once at a pot luck dinner they had at the fire station. Sammy invited the kids and I went to drop them off and he insisted I stay. Sammy was very well liked and got along great with all of his co workers. He had a quality about him that was gentle and sweet. His mother was a small rather heavy gentle German lady with graying hair, her age was showing I assume from raising 4 children. I heard she was the best cook in the country. Sammy's father more of the rugged hard working type, his hair was almost white and he had calluses on his hands. I knew he had been a worker in his day. He was a mixture of Indian and Welch (go figure) never the less they were both extremely nice people. They told me they had lived n the same house since they married almost 60 years ago. They thought the world of Sammy and his brother. They are a very close family.

Sammy had two older sisters but each lived in a different state, miles away and he didn't get to see them very often. Sara who is 52 is his oldest sister had 2 boys both in collage now that he has seen a total of 5 times. Kathy is 49 --- still single and loving it Sammy says. She's just not the marring type. She's too independent. He's mentioned before he would love to see them. *"OMG"* I said out loud he will see them but it will be for a horrible reason, the death of their brother. I wouldn't wish this on anyone. Boy I wasn't looking forward to meeting them at all not under these circumstances.

This had to be a tough time on Sammy. He was putting up with Shelly and me and then his brother. I wouldn't want to go through any of this.

The funeral was to be this coming Friday and I wasn't looking forward to it at all. We were to meet at the cemetery. We didn't think it was good for the kids to go so I was glad they were in school. When I got there I could see

Sammy with his arm around his mother. She may have had gray hair but not a hair was out of place. She wore a dark blue suit that fit her frame perfectly. She looked stunning I thought to myself. I stood off to the back as I didn't want to interfere. I wasn't feeling good and was light headed but I wanted to go.

Sammy was looking around as if to be looking for someone. He spotted me and came over quickly and pulled me to the front with his sisters and mom and dad. I gave my condolences to the family. The guys Sammy worked with were there and so many other people. It was a beautiful service but at the end it started to rain and lightning like it hadn't done in a long time. Sammy looked up at the sky and said. "Well bro that was some departure. I love you and will miss you terribly" With that I felt the tears come to my eyes. We went to his Mom & Dad's house for a while then I had to leave to get the kids. I was not feeling good at all and needed to go home and rest.

"I'll be over later." Sammy said.

"Take your time, your family needs to be together right now. Just call me later please,

OK?" I amswered quitly. He shook his head and gave me a little grin. I really just wanted to get back to bed and rest. He wanted to drive me home and I said "No I'm ok you go be with your family."

CHAPTER 13

I MUST HAVE DOZED off as soon as I got home from picking up the kids. I woke the next morning thirsty, very thirsty. I don't remember anything all night. I tried to get out of bed and was dizzy so I laid back down. Jason was at the door asking if I was OK. "Sure honey, I'll be all right" "Jason, do you think you can you get me a glass of water?" "Ya" with that he bounced off to the kitchen before I could tell him to not fill it up all the way. When he returned I was surprised to see he had the glass on my wooden tray.

"Thank you sweetie--- the tray was a good idea."

"I saw you do it, member."

"Yes I remember when we had Clara over for tea right."

" uh hu" he replied.

"Thank you so much Jason that was really a smart idea, that way you don't spill it."

"uh, well I pill in the chi-chichn." he tried so hard to say the works right but they just won't come out.

"It's ok we'll get it picked up later." "Want to get up here with me and we'll watch some cartoons."

"Ya," he said jumping up on the bed as fast as he could. He snuggled up next to me and watched cartoons for about an hour. I found out later that Shelly had kept him occupied and watched him the night before. Sammy was worried and came over so she handled him for an hour and I guess did pretty good.

I had taken my pain pills and was getting sleepy but I didn't want to go to sleep again with Jason here alone, I couldn't exactly depend on Shelly right now. I hadn't heard any movement from here room yet so I guessed she was still asleep. The front door opened and I assumed it was Sammy, but it wasn't. I felt so vulnerable right them. My head was spinning and a stranger in my house. A lady called out my name a couple of times and I thought she must know me.

"Hello," I said and she appeared in the door way of my room.

"Hi, I'm Dee Dee a friend of Sammy's," she said as she came into the room. He asked me to check in on you. His parents are so upset over the loss of Stan that Sammy was worried about leaving. He asked me to come over and see if I can get you anything until he felt it was ok to leave his folks."

"That's really nice of you. Thanks. I'm a bit dizzy when I try to get up and really could use something to drink. I'm so dry," Jason had fallen back to sleep. She picked up the prescription bottle and said, "It's because of these they make you thirsty all the time."

"And there not helping much with the pain either. But they sure make me sleepy." I replied.

I watched her as she read the label on the bottle; she was a very pretty woman about 35 and had the most beautiful brown hair. Long and flowing like the TV commercials you see. You know those gorgeous lady's the ones where they throw their head back and their hair goes swinging back n forth. Her completion was perfect --- she had the longest eye lashes. *I think I hate her already for these beautiful traits......* I wondered if Sammy was seeing her, maybe they were engaged. He hadn't said anything to me, but then we hadn't seen that much of each other in the past year. I was busy with the kids and they were full time with the activities after school, home work, etc. Sammy was a coach of the local high school baseball team, elementary soccer team and went to the YMCA once a week to help out. That and his work kept him tied up. So we had both been very busy since we had met a little over 3 years ago.

She seemed nice and I really was glad she was here to help. I ask her to go check on Shelly since I hadn't heard from her. She didn't come back for few minutes and when she did she said she had been all over the house and outside and couldn't find her. "Oh no, not again." I said with tears starting to form in my eyes.

Sammy had told Dee Dee that I was having a little trouble with Shelly so she was concerned. I was too! Where had she gone and when did she leave? After what had happened I was so worried about her. I need to get her into someone she can talk to. Someone who will tell her she's ok and nothing that has happened is her fault. I can't seem to get through to her. I have tried but just don't have the experience to tell her what she wants to hear.

Dee Dee looked concerned and asks "Should we call Sammy? Or maybe call the police?" I don't know I hated to bother Sammy at a time like this so I decided to call 911. "Hello, what is you emergency?" the lady ask as if she was in a real hurry.

"My daughter is missing,"
"What is your name and address and phone number." She seemed to growl, As I was telling her she interrupted and said. "How old is she?" "Has she ever run away before?"
"Is she pregnant?"
"10, No, No. "
"How long has she been gone?"
"I don't know!"
"You don't know?"

"I was sick and--"

"Lady you should always know where your children are at all times."

"Give me a description of her." That's when I lost it and Dee Dee took the phone.

"Yes, I'm a friend and I want you to know you have really offended this woman she just got home from the hospital 2 nights ago and Shelly was here. A friend was staying with them but was called out on the shooting at the mall. He was then presented with seeing his brother lying dead from a gunshot in front of him. So we have been just a little hectic around here. So please loose the attitude and help us find Shelly." "I'm sorry to hear that, just a minute---I'll get you with an officer." Dee Dee handed me back the phone and said someone would be over here shortly. "I'm going to go outside and look around some more you talk to the officer." With that she seemed to glide out the door like a model. How jealous I was to see such a beautiful woman and knowing she was such a good friend of Sammy's. I wondered how long they knew each other? Had they had a relationship? Just how close were they? Lots of questions. But not now---she was a God send to me. I don't know what I would have done without her here.

CHAPTER 14

I WAITED WHAT seemed like hours on the phone but it was only minutes. I was irritated, I know the police are busy but when a child is missing you would think they would be a little faster at answering the phone.
"Hello this is Officer Bailey what can I do for you?" "My name is Amy Grant I'm sorry, I said while choking up (it was hard to talk without crying) and my daughter Shelly is missing."
"OK how old is she and give me a description of her."

"She just turned 10 a couple of months ago and has brownish blond hair." "Slow down is it brown or blond?"

"Like I said it is a brownish blond. "She's about 4' tall and is slender build. She has a promenade scar on her forehead under her bangs."

"Where did she get the scare?" he asks with a funny tone to his voice.

"She was in a car accident when she was smaller, if you must know." "Hey." he said. We get all kinds down here I had to ask."

Then he added do you have a recent picture of her and have you checked friends, neighbors, around the house?"

"I wouldn't be calling you now if I hadn't already called everyone she or I know." " What is wrong with you people will someone please go look for her."

"Calm down lady I'm getting to that." "Not fast enough!" I added. This guy was as bad as the lady who first answered the phone.

He took my name and address and told me he would send an officer out to talk to me. Most of the time he said the kids weren't missing just visiting someone and didn't tell me.

I put the phone back on the cradle and sat staring out the window. The police are supposed to make you feel better but after this call I felt worse.

Shelly was in so much trouble. I think I'll ground her for the rest of her life. How could she do this again? I had tried so hard to be there for her and she was treating me as if I was her enemy. "Dear God, I'm not much at praying but please let her be ok and come home soon. I don't know what I'd do if something bad happened to her."

I can't remember the last time I prayed or if I ever have. This was a real prayer and I hoped God would answer me with the return of Shelly.

The tears started flowing again as Dee Dee came into the room and said she had no luck. She had gone to all the neighbors and no one had seen her. "I think we should call Sammy" she said in a low sympathetic voice. "No I can't do that he just lost his brother he needs to be with his family right now."

There was a knock on the door, Dee Dee said "I'll get it" I overheard her say yes, come in she's in the living room. A very tall black headed officer about 40 years old came in and introduced himself as Officer Kenny. "If you don't mind I'd like to ask you some questions." "That's *fine but why aren't you out looking for Shelly?"*

"There has been an alert put out to all of the area. They are looking for her now. But if you have a picture I'm sure it will go faster. Here are a lot of kids who fit you're daughters description." Dee Dee's hand was on my shoulder. "If you tell me where it is I'll get it for you."

"On the buffet in the large picture frame it's this year's school picture. It's only a month old so it looks just like her."

Dee Dee took the picture out of the frame and handed it to Officer Kenny. He looked at it and said, "nice looking little girl. She's not smiling in the picture." I looked at him and quickly replied "I know she's unhappy & embarrassed by her scar---she doesn't smile much." "She's not happy at home?" He asked.

I answered, raising my voice a bit. "She is." He came back with "Sorry but we need to know things like this. It can give us a ideal of whether she may be a run away. Or maybe she's just mad at the family and wanting attention. Not every child is like that but, believe me there are a lot of troubled kids who don't think about how worried the family can be."

His last comment did make me feel a little less guilty. I thought it was a good idea to open up to him; it may help in their search for her. "Officer Kenny, I honestly don't know what she's capable of right now, she's going through some tough times. Her mother was killed in the accident and she misses her so much. She's been getting worse in the last 6 months or so."

"How did you come about getting her? Are you a relative?" " No-no I was at the scene when the accident---when it happened. It was right outside my front door. Her mother asks me to take them in and raise them since she had no living family. The father had died in a fire along with both of her parents. Their father's parents died a long time before that.

"Take them in? You just took them in and started taking care of them? Raising them as your own?" He asks. "Yes I know it sounds crazy but I took in Shelly and her brother. They are my kids now and I love them dearly." I said.

"Oh you adopted them? Or do you have guardianship?" he asked.

Right then my heart sunk "Well no, not exactly." I said with my voice quivering. *What was he getting at? They were already enrolled in school and I just took over as mother…….No one had ever questions me before.*

Dee Dee was looking at me with a strange look and said. "Ok I think you have had enough questions let's get you back in bed." She turned to the officer and told him I had just gotten out of the hospital and needed to rest. She helped me to my room and into bed. She said she would be right back after she let Officer Kenny out.

She appeared at the door with a troubled look on her face. "Sweetie we need to talk. Can I ask you a couple of questions?"

"Yes, go ahead." I mumbled.

"Ok, let's start at the beginning. You were at the scene of an accident and a lady asked you to take her kids and raise them, right?"

"Yes"

"Did you ever apply for or get adoption or legal guardianship of either child?"

"My God no, what have I done? How could I be so stupid? I was a career woman I worked with legal issues every day. How could I have forgotten something so important? No one has ever questioned it before."
Dee Dee added. "Look, don't get so upset I know a lawyer, as a matter of fact I'm dating him. I will ask him what your best options are and we'll get this cleared up ok?" Don't you worry. Just get some rest now and I'll take care of things."

My head was reeling what was going on. In all of the commotion of trying to be the best mother I could be--- had I forgotten to do what was legal? The most important thing of all, *'adopt them'*.....I was shaking terribly, his comments really hit hard.

I hadn't thought about it before. What would happen now? Would they or could they take my kids away from me? *Little did I know how much I had screwed up and what was about to happen........*

CHAPTER 15

IT WAS GETTING DARK and they hadn't found Shelly. I was so worried. Dee Dee had taken Jason to let me rest. How could I rest not knowing where she was or if she was hurt? I was a basket case. My head was pounding, stomach hurt, I was nauseated.

There was a knock at the door but I couldn't get up very fast. I slowly made my way to the door balancing myself on the hall wall me and the kids had painted last year. It turned out pretty good a nice shade of yellow which brightened the hallway up. I had also bought the kid friendly paint. (Jason didn't always wash his hands as good as he should have. Shelly on the other hand was a clean freak. She washed hers before and after a meal, after we came back from Dr's, mall, park or wherever we had been.) As I approached the door I could see through the glass on the door it was Officer Kenny.

"Oh god, have you found her?" I ask.

"Uh would it be possible to have you come down to the station? We uh have found a girl matching Shelly's description but it's hard to tell from the picture."

"What, how could you not tell from the picture she looks just like the school photo?" *Just then Dee Dee and Jason walked up.*

Dee Dee said, "What's up?" "They um found a girl and can't tell by the photo if it's Shelly.. God just ask her, she'll own up to it and tell you."

"We can't do that miss." I looked at him and it hit me................

I don't remember much more I passed out and woke up on the couch with Sammy looking over me.

"Sweetheart it's not her, It's not Shelly." I went

down to the police department and saw her…
it's not Shelly. Dee Dee called me when
you passed out. It's not Shelly."

"Thank God, Sammy I was so scared. Did Dee
Dee tell you about the adoption? Did she tell
you I may lose both Shelly and Jason. (my
voice raising as I spoke)" What am I going to
do? How could I be so stupid?"

"Yes she told me; don't worry about
anything we will get through this I promise.
It was an oversight." He   said. "Just   calm
down everything will be ok."

I looked at the pain in his eyes and said. "I
didn't want to take you away from your
family, I'm so sorry." I said with a crack in my
voice. I knew Sammy was still mourning the
loss of his brother. I could see hurt in his eyes.

"I told you if you ever needed me to call no
matter what, well this is a time you should have
called. I needed to be here to help you.
But right now we need to find Shelly."

Dee Dee had taken Jason to the kitchen
so we could talk. He was happy as long as he
had his cookies and milk. Sammy looked me
straight in the eyes and said, "look I've got to
say this and I know it may not be the right time

but I fell head over heels in love with you the first time I saw you. I want you to know whatever happens I will be there for you." I was stunned and just stared at him. "I'm sorry I shouldn't have said that, I was out of line."

Oh Sammy I fell in love with you too! I didn't know it till right now but I have been in love with you since I first met you."

He replied with. "We've wasted so much time. When I get back we will talk and figure out where to go from here, ok? "

"Ok Sammy, that sounds great." With that he leaned over and gave me a long lingering kiss. "Ok now I'm going to find Shelly and bring her home. You stay right here and wait for me. I'll find her."

I waited for what seemed like hours for Sammy to bring Shelly back. Finally I heard his car in the driveway. Staring at the door I waited impatiently for it to open. When I saw Shelly and Sammy enter I was so relieved I wanted to scream. Shelly looked so tired. "Shelly, come here." She slowly walked over to me---bent down and said. "I didn't mean to scare you I just didn't feel like I was part of your family. It hurt me to see you paying so much attention to

Jason."

"Shelly honey, I love you both very much ---I have to tend to Jason more because he's so little. He can't do what you can he just isn't old enough yet."

"I know that now, I had a long talk with Sammy and he said you were so worried."

"I was I really was. I'm so glad your home safe. Sit down here next to me and let's talk a bit while Dee Dee is putting Jason to bed."

Sammy told me she was at a culvert where a couple of other kids were. They were all talking about how bad their lives were and when he got there she had realized she didn't have it so bad after all. One of the boys named Frankie had a mother who did crack and hit him all the time. He was so bruised up Shelly tried to get him to tell someone but he didn't have anywhere else to go so he was sticking it out. She would bring guys home and they would push him around and make him get them beer and drugs from the closet. Once a guy had hit his mom so hard he thought she was dead, Frankie had stayed out of school and nursed her till she was better. When it got really bad he would go to the culvert. He could hide there and no one cared if he was in school or not.

The girl Samantha had an abusive step father who was doing what she called nasty things to her. She couldn't stand it but had nowhere to go. She once told her mother but she didn't believe her so she just kept quiet about it after that. She said one day she was going to kill her step father and then he would leave her alone.

I couldn't believe what I was hearing. What would happen to these kids and why wasn't anyone helping them. I looked over at Sammy and saw the look of someone who was shocked and sad.

My first priority was to adopt Shelly and Jason then maybe I could help some of these kids. I was determined to try. The attorney I talked to said it could take a while because of having to wait for the death certificate on their mother, dad and grandparents. We had to have all of them. Plus we had to show the kids had no living relatives.

CHAPTER 16

WHEN SHELLY WENT to bed Sammy and I talked. It was as if we had been together all our lives and were solving a problem that had come up. We were so in touch with each other. I just don't know how I couldn't have seen it. I knew there was some feeling for him but didn't know how much until we talked that night.

About a week later Sammy came to dinner and really surprised me. "I really do love you very much and I want to be with you forever. I don't want you to have to go through what you've been through alone again. Sweetheart (Sammy said as he got down on one knee and pulled a small box out of his pants pocket) will you do me the honor of being my wife?" Shocked, yes to say the least--- happy, you bet!

"Yes I will ---I love you Sammy so very much. I want to be with you forever too." Again that long lingering kiss that had sent firecrackers off earlier.

Wow--- it's all happening so fast yet it's been so long coming. I couldn't wait to tell Shelly and Jason we were going to be a complete family. I fell asleep that night the happiest person on earth. My life was complete, I was ecstatic.

We were all at the table the next morning Shelly, Jason, Dee Dee, Sammy and me, when I ask Sammy if I could tell everyone. "If you don't I'll be disappointed." I looked at him smiling. "Go ahead tell them." He said.

"Ok listen up everyone. Sammy has ask me to marry him and I said......YES!" There was a silence that came over the room and I was becoming scared of it lasting too long. Finally Dee Dee jumped in (thank Goodness and broke the silence) "Well, I think that's great .Congratulations to both of you. I'm so happy for you."

"Thank You!" we both said at the same time. Jason popped up with, "wuts dat mean." I looked over at Shelly and she appeared to be pouting. She answered him with a sarcastic tone, "It means they're going to be together now. They're going to live together. Just them two. That means we will be alone and have to go to an orphanage and live. We may not even be together." She was getting so upset. She was about to leave the table.

Sammy looked over at her with so much love in his eyes and said. *"Shelly--- it means we are going to be a real family.* You, Jason, Mom and me. We're going to look for a bigger house, if that's ok with mom. One that's our home as a family. With a big yard---bigger swing set, maybe even a dog. You can choose the color of your rooms again if you want. How does that sound?"

"Are you serious?" Shelly came back with. Shelly got up and gave me a big hug.

"Yes I am serious. We have been apart way to

long---it's time we became the family we were meant to be." Jason was up bouncing around saying doggy, doggy, doggy. Ya, Ya, Ya....

Shelly put both her hands on each side of my checks and said "I'm really happy now." Someone pinch me was this happening to me? I could feel the tears in my eyes. I rushed to blink them back. I knew if I started I would be crying for a while. I wanted to enjoy the moment. Remembering again back not too long ago at how my life had been. How does a person go from one extreme to the other in just a few short years? It has been a good extreme turnaround and I wouldn't change a thing. I have grown so much as a person.

Sammy and I started making plans for the wedding. We were going to wait for a period of time since Stan had just been buried. We started planning though for the big day. Sammy wanted to have a large wedding with all the trimmings. I was a bit more conservative since I knew it was going to take a lot of money. I did want a beautiful wedding dress but that was my only requirement was that it didn't cost an arm and a leg. I wanted to be able to hand it down to Shelly.

Dee Dee and I have become very good friends since that night and she has helped me so much with the wedding plans. She went with me to pick out my dress and it is beautiful. I chose a form fitting beauty with long sleeves and high neckline, sequins and pearls. It has long train with a large veil with sequins and pearls along the edge, with white satin shoes with delicate pearls to match. I was so excited. When Dee Dee saw me in it I knew it was the one. It brought tears to her eyes

"You look absolutely gorgeous. This dress was made for only you."

"Thanks Dee Dee I love it. Do you think Sammy will like it?"

"How could he not like it you look exquisite in it. Honestly it was made for you."

"I'm so happy Dee Dee I could scream." She just stood back a bit and smiled at me.

"Now that I have chosen this one I ask the saleslady "how much is this dress? It was the only one without a price tag.

I was holding my breath because I wanted it so badly. "Let's see it doesn't seem to have a tag on it, I'll be right back." She went to the front counter to check the price and I watched her as she picked up the phone. I wanted her to get rid of that customer so I could be happy or heartbroken. Thought I had done just what I didn't want to do. Chosen a dress had no idea what the cost was. I really wanted to stay around $800.00. I don't know if this beautiful gown was even going to come close to that.

As she returned I saw a look in her eye as she said. "I know you wanted to stay in $ 800.00 range, so what would you say if I told you this beautiful dress that looks so good on you is (she hesitated for a minute) $799.00."
"Oh my God--- are you kidding me?"
"No, that's the price to you."
"I'll take it now please. No alterations it fits perfect."
"Yes I see that--- we usually have to alter. But this dress was made for you." I looked at Dee Dee and she and I started laughing. *Yes it was made just for me........*

CHAPTER 17

SAMMY AND I HAD planned the wedding for June 10. He said there's just something about a June wedding that just seems right. We picked a venue in an old Victorian House down on State Street. I had always loved this house the old time charm, design, architecture. It was perfect. I drove past it every day when I was working at the office. There was always something so special about this old house.

The stair case comes down in the center

of the entry which had a huge chandelier hanging from the 12' ceilings. This chandelier had to be 3 foot wide. It was absolutely gorgeous and shined like stars in the night. The floors were done in marble so shiny you can see yourself in them---the wood trim and baseboards were a medium Oak with a marble fireplace mantle to die for. The couple who owned the house had converted it to do weddings in---the court yard is for the reception with walls of roses all colors around the lush green yard. A large 5 tier water fountain is circled by more roses and statues. There were lights everywhere. It is truly magnificent.

The owners handled everything including the catering, drinks, brides room, grooms room, Music everything but the champagne glasses and cake. Oh and the cake is going with the theme of roses. It's a 4 tier white cake with yellow roses and green leaves cascading down the side. It has the bride and groom on top with a little girl for Shelly and little boy for Jason standing on each side of the couple.

Shelly is going to be the flower girl and Jason the ring bearer, following their walk down the aisle they will both stand at the altar with us for we are all becoming one on this special day. We would all stand in front of the minister and take our vows.

Our day was fast approaching when I had a thought. After looking for a home for about 4 months we finally found what we considered the perfect house. We had made an offer on a 5 bedroom home with a huge yard not far from where we live now. It was only 3 years old and had been very well taken care of. It had new appliances, carpet and paint. I was supposed to hear back from the realtor ---she had not called yet. I pulled over to the curb and gave her a call. "Oh yes how are you dear?" she said in her very quiet voice. "I'm fine, I was just wondering if you heard back on our offer." "You know I haven't." She answered. "But let me call the other realtor and I'll call you right back." I told her thanks as I hung up. We really think this house will be perfect for all of us and the kids both love it and can't wait to move in. I do hope they accept our offer. The only drawback I have is it's two stories; I'm not fond of the stairs. I could see myself running up and down them every day chasing the kids.

Not!

The phone rang and it was her, she said the owners are coming back with a counter offer but not to worry it's nothing major. "Great you will call me as soon as you hear won't you?" "I certainly will dear you have a good day." With that we hung up and I continued on to the cleaners to pick up some things. As I approached the cleaners I noticed what looked like a teenager running out of the jewelry store next to the cleaners. He was in a hurry stumbling over an old couple maybe in their 80's --- pushing the woman to the ground. She fell hard---I knew she had to be hurt. I jumped out of the car to see if I could help when bam I was knocked down. I was so busy looking at the couple I hadn't noticed the teenager was headed straight for me.

I started to get up and this little punk grabbed my keys which I had dropped on the ground and took off in my car almost running over me. Boy that didn't make my day. How dare him. I still had my cell phone in my hand so I dialed 911.

"What's your emergency?" came from the dispatcher who sounded like she was having a real bad day.

"Some kid just knocked down me and old lady then stole my car. He's headed down Center Street."

"What kind of car and the license plate number?" she asked.

"It's a silver Chevy Tahoe I don't know the license plate number. It's my friend Sammy's SUV he's a fireman here in the valley."

"Ok I have an officer on the way, please stay on the line till he gets there."

"You need to send a paramedic."

"Are you hurt?" replied the 911 voice

"No, but he knocked a lady and her husband to the ground as he was running, I don't know about the old man but the lady fell to the ground really hard. She may be hurt." I got up and went over to where the lady was and saw she was bleeding from the side of her head and not moving too much.

There was a crowd and I heard someone say the boy had robbed the jewelry store.

"I saw him running out of the store with a bag in his hand and a guy chasing him." The man yelled. Waving his hands about like a mad man. He was telling this story over and over to anyone who would stop and listen.

I asked a couple of people there if the man was ok and they said ya he was sitting in front of the building. I went over to him and he said he was ok. I told him I called the paramedic and they would be here shortly. He thanked me and I heard the wailing of sirens coming down the street. Ear piercing sirens I hated the sound of sirens it brings back bad memories.

I felt a hand rest on my shoulder, it was Sammy. The fire department responded too. They always do when there's report of an accident.

"What are you doing here?" he asked.

"I was coming to the cleaners when this teenager ran into this lady then into me and stole your car."

"You're kidding right"

"No, do I look like I'm kidding? He really did. I called the police and there looking for him. Some guy said he robbed the jewelry store." "Are you ok? Hey you're arms bleeding too. Guys need someone over here too" he yelled out at the paramedics.

"I'm ok it's just a scratch." I replied.

"Humor me, let em look at it ok?"

"Ok"

"Gotta go---see ya at dinner tonight." he said as he went to see if he could help. He loved his job and he was good at it. He had been with the fire department over 10 years.

I ended up with a bandage and a sore arm and elbow, but Sammy's Tahoe was still not found. I would have to get a rental since my car was in the shop and I had so much to do with the wedding---so close. Then there's the house we made an offer on. I would have paperwork on it. *If we can come to terms on it.*

CHAPTER 18

AFTER TAKING A CAB home I was remembering the teenager who had run into me. I gave the police a description as best I could. I did look him in the eye just before he ran into the lady and a full description of my car, including all the groceries new cloths for the kids that were in it. I didn't have Shelly's dress yet but I had just bought Jason's suit. Plus I had just filled it up with gas. I'm sure I won't get that back. Oh no my wedding dress was in the back. My beautiful gorgeous dress was packed so neatly in the back.

Ringgggggg off went the phone. "Hello"
"Dear, guess what the owners have changed their mind and have accepted your offer as is." The real estate lady said.
"Oh that's great, you just made my bad day turn good."
"I'm so glad. We can get together today to sign the papers if you like."
"That's fine Sammy will be off work at 2:30 and home by 3pm how's 3:30 sound?"
"Good dear 3:30 pm it is, I'll see you then. Goodbye dear."

The kids won't be home for another two hours so I thought I'd lie down for a while. I was sore and tired. As soon as I hit the bed I was asleep. I was woken up an hour later by some rattling in the kitchen. It was Sammy making dinner. He was a great cook and I loved it when he took over like that. He was so busy I hated to bother him. He looked up and saw me and rushed over and said "are you ok?"
"I'm OK just still mad at that kid, how could he do that to someone so fragile?"
"I know some people just don't care, sit down this is about ready."
"Oh I forgot to call you, what time is it?"

"It's 4:00 why?"

"We were to meet the realtor on the house to sign the papers they accepted our offer." "Great well that must have been the phone message I got saying that she wouldn't be able to make it and wanted to schedule for tomorrow at the same time. She wanted us to call and confirm."

"Ok I'll call her now." As I went to the phone I told Sammy I wanted to go out tomorrow and look for his Tahoe. "I feel so bad he took your SUV." As I mumbled to myself I looked around and saw a mess. I need to pick up some of this stuff before one of us get hurt stumbling over it. "Don't worry about it I have good insurance on it." He replied as I left the room. I was looking for my book with all of my phone numbers and appointments--- I remembered they were in the SUV. Great I thought, that book had a lot of information in it. "Sammy I have to tell you something. My wedding dress was in the car. I don't know if I can ever find one like it again. It was so perfect. I just love it and loved wearing it." "Don't worry sweetheart we'll find another one just like it." Sammy said with sympathy in his voice.

As we were watching TV that night the phone rang. It was the police

"May I speak to Amy Grant?" said a man with a very husky voice.

"I'm Amy Grant"

"This is Officer Perry and I wanted to call and let you know we found your SUV."

"Great thanks for calling when can we pick it up?" I asked.

"Well there's a problem with that, you see it was used in a robbery and it is being held for evidence." After he said that there was a silence.

"But I need it. It has all of my paperwork in it. It has my wedding dress. My beautiful wedding dress, I'm getting married and..."

He cut me off quickly with "Congratulations miss!"

"Thank you but you don't understand I have clothes, papers for work phone numbers I need in that car." I sprang at him.

"Look, I'm sorry there's nothing I can do it's in the impound yard. They won't let it go until it's cleared. Can you understand that?" He came back with almost shouting.

"Great!" I said as I was looking at Sammy and the kids wondering what was happening. "Thanks for calling." I said and hung up.

Sammy asked if that was the police and I told him what they said. "I'm sorry I didn't mean to get your car stolen."

"I know Amy don't worry about it maybe it won't take long, I have rental insurance so I'll have you take me in the morning to get a car. As for the things you had in there well there probably gone anyway."

I just shook my head and headed into the kitchen to make the popcorn. We were watching a movie Jason wanted to get. Then it would be off to bed for him and Shelly. So far Shelly was being a little angel. I hadn't had any trouble out of her at all and it was real peaceful. She didn't argue about going to school like she did every morning a while back. She helped me around the house and even did laundry. I couldn't ask for more as long as she stayed that way we would get along just fine.

The wedding was getting closer and I was getting nervous. I hadn't found a wedding dress. The one I planned on wearing had been soiled with something that wouldn't come out.

It was ruined. The insurance company covered the cost of it but I can't find another one anywhere. I don't feel comfortable in anything else.

Our house went through and we were moving the weekend after the wedding. Sammy was taking me to Italy for our honeymoon. I had mentioned how beautiful it was and wanted to go back someday. I wanted all of us to experience the new house together. Dee Dee said she would stay with the kids while we were gone. I had packed all that I wanted to take. The rest I was going to donate. I wanted to start fresh. New house new furniture new husband and new family.

While I sat at the table one day I was daydreaming of a flower garden with yellow Calla Lilies and yellow roses lining the brick wall,climbing all the way to the top of it. I could see a beautiful fountain in the middle of the yard somewhat like the one at the venue we were getting married at. I wanted a place for a garden so I could grow all of our vegetables. *'Boy listen to me I sound like a house wife, WOW that's what I want to be. Am I crazy?* No I thought it's just that I have changed so much.

I didn't even recognize myself.

I got up to get another cup of coffee and the phone rang. "Ouch" I screamed as I hit the edge of the table as I reached to get the phone. *'Man that hurt.'* "Hello"

"Hi, is this Amy Grant?" A quiet voice said as if she was afraid to speak.

"Yes, this is her can I help you?" I shot back while still babying a hurt toe.

"My name is Stella, Stella Forth. I was just wondering if this is the Amy Grant who used to live in South Dakota?" I hesitated and couldn't imagine who knew where I was from.

"May I know why you want to know"

There was a bit of a silence and then she hung up. *'Boy that was strange'* I thought as I hung up the phone. I couldn't figure out who it might be. It puzzled me all afternoon. But the next day was busy so I didn't give it any more thought.

CHAPTER 19

 I HAD ERRANDS to run the next day so I started early. I had been to a few different places when I noticed I had seen the same car blue minivan with a dented driver's side door everywhere I had been. I saw a small woman in the driver's seat. She was a red head with her shoulder length hair flowing and rather a pretty lady. She had a pair of red and white sunglasses on that looked to be way too big for her. When she saw I was looking at her she started the car and took off. That was strange the way she acted it was like she had been following me and suddenly got caught.

I had to stop at the attorneys on the adoption of Shelly and Jason. I have to say it wasn't going very fast. Sammy and I were both going to adopt them. The paperwork was so pilling up on us. I think we have answered a million questions and signed a couple thousand papers. He told me there had been a snag in the adoption. It seems there's a lady who claims to be a relative of Shelly and Jason.

"That's impossible their mother told me there weren't any living relatives left." I told him.

"Well she has filed papers with the court for full custody." "What?!" I shot back. This couldn't be happening. Not now not after such a long time. I was stunned and left in a daze hoping this all wasn't real.

I did the rest of my errands and headed home. I was tired so I took a short nap before Jason got home from school. Shelly was staying over at a friend's to do some homework and wouldn't be home till later so it was just Jason and me for dinner. That was nice because anything that had hot dog in it was Ok with Jason. I didn't have to cook a big dinner anyway.

I went to the door as Jason was getting off the bus and saw that same minivan down the street on the other side. *'What is going on'* I said out loud. "What?" Jason said. I looked down at him and said, "nothing sweetie how was your day?"

"Okie dokie I guess." That's what he said every day. Okay Dokie. I just smiled but as I looked up and down the street the minivan was gone again. Now I'm getting mad. Why would someone be watching me? Could it be the lady the attorney had told me about? I had to get to the bottom of this and see who she really was.

I told Sammy about what the attorney had said and he was speechless. "You know I have seen a blue minivan around the fire house lately. It had a lady in it. She took off when she noticed I was looking at her."

"It has to be the same lady." I said as I was trying to think how long has, she been watching us.

"What are we going to do Sammy?"

"I don't know I guess go to court and see what she has to say."

"I don't want to lose the kids, we've come so far and they're happy here."
Sammy replied with. "I know, I know don't worry we'll figure something out."
I could see the look of worry in his eyes as he leaned over and kissed me goodnight and I walked him to the door. This could be a big problem. We could lose the kids forever. I can't let that happen.

Our attorney Mr. Archer who was a small gray haired man with a small mustache and slight beard, called the next day to tell us we were due in court in a week. That was the longest week we had ever spent. We had two meetings with Mr. Archer that lasted a couple of hours each. He wanted to know everything that had happened since Jason and Shelly had come to live with me. I tried to remember everything but I probably left some stuff out. I or I should say Sammy and I weren't thinking to straight these days. He wanted to know all good and bad things so there would be no surprises in court. He said,
"I know the other attorney and believe me she does her homework. If anyone can dig up dirt it's her." We tried not to talk about it thinking

that the lady may go away, but she hadn't so we prepared for court.

The day of court we all went into the court room and I saw the same lady that had been watching us. We found out it was a distant cousin of Shelly and Jason's father. She had finally found the kids and wanted custody of them. Our attorney fought and told the judge the kids had been with us for so long it wasn't right to just yank them away. They had been so traumatized by all of the deaths in the family it could hurt them emotionally.

The lady's attorney stated she was a blood relative and she wanted to see them. Then she brought up the police report of Shelly missing and that didn't look good. She kept talking about it and the judge was listening to her every word.

"I hate to say it but I think that was going to hurt our case." Said Mr. Archer while making notes as if to tell us we screwed. I wasn't very happy with either him or the court system right now.

The judge said he would take everything under advisement and let the attorney's know of his decision in the mail.

"Decision in the mail, do you believe that." I ask Sammy. "How can one person make a decision like that in the mail?" "I don't know Amy, I just don't know." He was very quite the rest of the way home so I didn't say anything either. We rode in silence.

It had been a couple of weeks and we had not heard from the attorney. While I washed the dishes from breakfast I was wondering why it was taking so long. I was thinking about calling him when the phone rang. It was indeed the attorney. He didn't sound very good and I got worried he kept saying little things like you know we knew we were going to have a hard time in court, and I sure wish the laws were different then he added I'm so sorry I tried but there was nothing I could do. "Wow what did you just say? Tell me I didn't hear that!" I screamed.

"I'm really sorry but the judge thinks the kids would be better off with a blood relative. You have to turn them over by noon tomorrow." "No, No, No, I can't do that they belong with me I promised their mother I would take care of them." As I started to cry I added, "She made me *pinky promise* with her then she died. I can't give them up. No, I won't give them up."

"Listen to me." he said. "You have to it's a court order they will throw you in jail if you don't comply. Don't do anything stupid."   By this time I was crying so hard it was getting hard to breathe. I found myself choking I was crying so hard and screaming at the same time. Thank God the kids weren't here, they were both still in school. I told the attorney I had to go and hung up.

After making coffee I sat down at the table looking out the window. *What was happening?* My whole life was falling apart before my eyes and I couldn't stop it. I didn't know what I was going to do. Sammy didn't know yet I was still crying and I knew I wouldn't be able to hold anything back when I told him. He would be home early today so I decided to wait til he got home. I had to think about what to do next. *I could take the kids and hide. I could plead with the relative God I didn't even know her name. Kathy I think.* Or I could take the job my boss Emily had offered me the other day. She wanted me to go back on the road. I would be traveling all over the country buying clothing lines from new and upcoming designers. I knew if I did that I wouldn't have time to think about the kids or Sammy.

CHAPTER 20

I WAS STILL SITTING at the table with so much going through my mind when Sammy came in. He bent over and kissed me then rose up to look at me when I didn't respond. "What's wrong Amy?" he asked.

I looked at him and he knew. "Mr. Archer called didn't he? Did he hear from the court? What did they say? Come on Amy tell me."

I cleared my throat and said, "Ya he called, and it wasn't good news. The judge feels they would be better off with a blood relative and we have to have Shelly and Jason at the court house tomorrow by noon." I was really breaking up but Sammy understood me. "Oh God." He sighed. He turned to look out the window. "That doesn't do any good I've been looking out that window since Mr. Archer called this morning."

"What you knew this morning and you didn't call me?"

"I knew it wouldn't do any good it wasn't going to change anything."

"No it wouldn't have but I wouldn't have spent another day wondering what was happening. Thanks a lot Amy nice going."

"Sorry I just didn't think it would do any good to call."

"That tells me a lot. Just what the hell do you think I'm here for? I need to know as much as you. We made a commitment to marry and take care of these kids I didn't know you had excluded me."

"Come on I didn't exclude you I just wasn't thinking, sorry ok?" I yelled as both of our voices were getting louder. Sammy stepped back a bit and gave me a look of disgust. I continued to look out the window not really caring what he thought. I need to decide what to do. Maybe I should have taken my job back when Denise called that day.

This was our first fight we had always gotten along great but these were trying times and the words just came out. What was bad was we weren't solving anything. The decision had been made by the court. I don't even know if we could appeal it.

He just stared at me and shook his head. " Ok I'm going home I have to think." He was mad.

"Sammy I'm sorry I should have called you." "I know you should have but you didn't." he said as he left the room. I heard the front door shut harder than usual and knew I had touched a very sore spot with him. All of our plans had been shattered and he was mad. Ok deal with it, I'm mad too.

The kids came in from school and I tried to act as normal as possible but Shelly knew there was something wrong. She kept asking me if I was Ok. "Yes sweetie I'm fine just tired I did a lot today." I finally got them off to bed and went back to the table. I sat at that same table til 3:00 in the morning with everything going through my head but I couldn't figure out what to do. I finally went in the bedroom---

took a shower to freshen up so the kids wouldn't know I was awake all night. I had breakfast ready the next day as usual trying to figure out how I was going to tell them.

I sat their plates on the table and told them they wouldn't be going to school. I had something to tell them and it wasn't going to be pretty. Shelly would know right away but Jason I would have explain everything to him.

Shelly had a worried look on her face as I started by telling them about the lady and then the day we went to court, finally the judge's decision. To my surprise Shelly just sat there and looked at me. Then she blurted out.

"Why didn't you tell us what was going on? We would have liked to know."

"I know but I didn't know how and I was hoping the lady would go away and forget about everything."

"Well she didn't--- did she?" Shelly said as she put her head in her hands pushed her hair back and said, "Well I knew it was too good to be true."

I looked over at Jason and he looked confused. I knew it was going to take some talking to get him to understand. I didn't know what else to say.

"Are you going to fight for us or are you going to let them take us away?" By this time Jason was crying. Shelly hadn't shed a tear.

"I don't know what I can do. I have to have you at the courthouse by noon and turn you over to your relative. I think her name is Kathy. She's a distant cousin of your dads. I don't want to Shelly believe me I don't want to. I thought about packing up and leaving but if I don't they will come after us no matter where we go. I just don't know what I'm going to do."

"Talk to the judge. I don't want to go with her." Still I saw no tears from Shelly. Jason was really crying and scared so I put him on my lap and hugged him trying to sooth him but it didn't do any good. He knew by now something was wrong.

"Shelly no matter what we do we have to have you and Jason at the court house by noon. I don't like this any more than you do. I'm going to be talking to everyone and try to get you both back."

"Ya--- pinky promise huh." She shouted as she left the room.

I took Jason up to his room and tried to

explain what was happening. He didn't understand why he and Shelly had to live with someone they didn't know. I told him I hoped it wouldn't be long that I was going to fight for him---I was going to get them back. I ask him to be a big boy (*I knew how much being a big boy meant to him.*) He said he would try after many tears and hugs. I didn't hear from Shelly til I told her we had to go.

She came out of her room with lots of makeup on. I usually told her to take some off but this time I figured she was trying to hide the evidence of crying. So I let her be I didn't want our last time together to be a fight. She came out of her room and flopped on the couch and said "I'm ready anytime." With that comment I didn't even respond. She wasn't going to get a fight out of me this was hard enough. We all loaded in the car and drove straight to the court house without the usual stopping for a drink of some kind---and we drove in silence. It was horrible. Even Jason didn't say anything.

CHAPTER 21

I PULLED THE CAR into a parking spot and when we all got out *with Jason still crying* I noticed Sammy standing on the huge set of steps going up to the door of the all marble courthouse. It was a beautiful building but right now I hated it more than any building I had ever seen. It was taking my babies away from me. *My babies that it seems were just on loan to me.* He came to meet us as we walked slowly along the brick path. My tears started again.

I wanted to run to him and put my arms around him and tell him my heart was breaking but I had to stay focused on Shell and Jason. He looked me right in the eye but didn't say anything. He took Shelly and Jason's hands and walked them up the steps to the extra large doors to the court house. We had to go through the motions of the scanner and taking everything out of our pockets.

When we were OK'd to go through I felt a ting of jealousy as I watched Shelly leaning against Sammy and holding onto his other arm for dear life. I felt guilty and left out. If I would have gone to court and adopted Shelly and Jason when they came to live with me the lady may not have ever known. How could I be so stupid?

We went into the court room and Shelly and Jason had to stay in the hall with an officer. The judge wasn't in the room but came in shortly after we entered and sat down.

"Is the third cousin of Shelly and Jason Jenson---Kathy Bracken in the court room today?" the judge said.

"Yes she is your honor *pointing to Kathy Bracken* and we are ready to proceed." Her attorney said. (She was a tall very thin woman with her bright red hair pulled back in a bun as

Items on Loan

Library name: Cloughfern
Library
User name: Karen Mahon

Author: Huff, Donna.
Title: Pinky promise
Mommy
Item ID: C900995678
Date due: 6/10/2015,23:59
Date charged: 15/9/2015,
12:42

Author: Harris, Rosie,
TBR5-Moving on
Item ID: C90117/475
Date due: 6/10/2015,23:59
Date charged: 15/9/2015,
12:42

LibrariesNI

tight as she could get it. She had a stunning tailored suit on that fit her very well. She looked stern—no mean, mad after blood.

"I have been over this case very many times and though I do sympathize with Miss Grant and the children by law I have to look at the overall situation. The children Shelly and Jason Jenson were put in Miss Grant's care at the request of her mother. I don't think Mrs. Jenson believed she had a choice as to who was to care for her children, and I'm not convinced had she known there was one living relative *Kathy Bracken* that she wouldn't have had the children sent to her. So it is the order of this court to award full custody to Kathy Bracken. This I believe is in the best interest of the children."

"Your honor if it pleases the court we would like to request some visitation. Shelly and Jason are very close to both Amy Grant and Sammy Jinson. They were both at the scene of the accident and visited both children in the hospital almost every day. I would like my petitions I filed with the court to grant them some kind of visitation. I have asked for certain dates but whatever the court feels justified then

I would leave it up to your honor." My attorney asked.

"I can see that they are very close and I don't want to harm the children any more than they have been harmed, so I will grant your petition for visitation. If I see t is harming the children then I will revoke it. Is that understood?"

"Yes your Honor that is very clear."

"Then that is the order of the court."

I could see that it didn't make Kathy Bracken very happy but I was just glad to be able to see them until I can figure out what to do. I thought to myself right now I will take anything I love those two kids so much I couldn't bear to not see them. Kathy Bracken's attorney seemed to be arguing with her--- I overheard her say she would talk to her in the hallway. We all got up and left the room. When we reached the hall around the corner where Shelly and Jason were being watched Jason ran to me. He was saying "I wove u don't want leave u. Wove u." It was heart wrenching and the tears came again as I held him in my arms and kissed him over and over again. I didn't want to let go but someone was tugging at him.

It was the officer asking me to let him go. "I love you Jason I'll see you soon." He was crying so hard. Shelly and Jason haven't even met this lady their going to be scared to death.

I could see Sammy hurting as he hugged Shelly and reached over and hugged Jason. I leaned down and gave Shelly a hug but she didn't hug back she wouldn't even look at me. She turned and went with Kathy and her attorney without even looking back. Jason was screaming by this time. They say *in the best interest of the child.* That was not in the best interest of any child. My heart was broken as I watched them being led away.

I sat down on the bench and cried and cried for the longest time. My heart was breaking and I didn't even have Sammy to lean on. He left as soon as they took Shelly and Jason away.

"Can I do anything to help?" asked an officer who saw me crying. "No thanks---no one can help now. Thanks anyway." I replied.

I got up and headed to the door. That was the longest walk I had ever made. I use to love the flowers at the courthouse but now I couldn't see them. It was all a blur. I got to my car and I honestly don't know how long I sat there. It was starting to get dark when I came out of the trance I had been in. I drove home and again it was a blur. I just wanted to get under the sheets and go to sleep so I could quite hurting.

CHAPTER 22

I TOOK THE longest drive home I had ever taken---don't remember much after that until I heard a loud banging at my front door. It startled me so much I hide under the covers. My first thought was ok great a home invasion that's all I need. After a couple of minutes I felt a tugging on my shoulder and looked up to see a fireman telling me the house next door was on fire and I need to go outside right now. I said let the house burn I don't care. After arguing with him for a short period of time he preceded to grab me and throw me over his shoulder and carry me out. I protested and screamed but it did no good he just kept walking very fast. My head was bobbing around like one of those bobble heads and the blood was rushing to it. I tried to wiggle out of his grip but he had such a firm hold on me I couldn't move. He put me on the ground by the street and said. "now stay there I'm going to be watching you."---I could see my neighbor's house blazing. Fire was coming out of what looked like every window in the house and through the roof. It was burning so fast. The fire trucks were spraying it as fast as they could but the house was going up to fast. I could feel the heat from the street where I sat in disbelief.

Then it hit me I wonder if Sammy is there. I didn't know his schedule at the time but he usually was called in on large fires. I didn't see him anywhere. All of a sudden I caught a whiff of myself. I don't remember the last time I showered. I don't even know how long I had been in bed and not gone out of the house. I didn't even know what day it was.

As I sat there watching the fire it was slowly coming back to me. The kids, the courthouse, Sammy, the judge...... Boy what a mess I had put everyone in by not doing the most important thing of all. *ADOPT THE KIDS.*

Bang!!! Bang!!! Ouch something just hit me. I kept hearing bangs. A policeman came over to me and said, "come on let's move that's live ammo going off." I got to my feet and he huddled me under his arm to protect me. We ran across the street and down a ways until he thought it was safe. "Sorry, I didn't want you to get hurt."

"I think I already did. Man anything else going to go wrong? My life has been a living hell."

"Let me see where are you hit?"

"In the shoulder." I answered.

"OK let's get you over to the paramedics so they can fix you up." He was an older policeman but very nice. He led me to the truck and sat me on the rear while telling the paramedics what had happened.

"You're lucky lady it just grazed your shoulder you'll be fine." The paramedic told me, while cleaning my wound and placing a patch on it. "Thanks, so you think I'm lucky huh? Well you don't know the half of it."

"All I know is about 1 ½ inches and the bullet would have hit your neck then you wouldn't have been so lucky." He looked at me and smiled and started picking up the mess from my wound.

"Thanks for the patch job." I said.

I watched the neighbors house go up so fast and burn to the ground. It didn't get near mine but at this time I wouldn't have cared. One of the officers said it would be a while before I could get back in my house. They wanted to make sure the flames were out. So I sat and watched for nearly 2 hours. Someone had given me a blanket to cover with and it felt good since it was a bit chilly.

My old image was to make sure I don't get to close to anyone. It was working pretty good for a while. Then the kids came into my life and I opened up not only to them but to Sammy. Look what it got me. I think I'm going to go back to my old image and not get close to anyone ever again. The pain wouldn't be there, the hurt, the feelings---the suffering. I had made up my mind to call my boss and take the job traveling again. That's the only way I can forget all that's happened.

When I was able to get back in the house the first thing I did was take a shower. I had to baby my shoulder and it hurt like crazy. I got through the shower ok and replaced the dressing with some new I had picked up at the store. It looked terrible but like the paramedic said I was lucky.

Boy the house was a real mess. I'll call Dottie she was the cleaning lady who helped me before while I was traveling. I'll need her again anyway. I needed to see what day it was and how long I had been out of it. When I finally found a calendar I saw it had been 9 days since I was in court. No wonder I could smell myself. The house reeked of foul food it was musty. I ran to the closet in the hall and got the air freshener and sprayed until I had used up the whole can. I decided I would start picking up---I could get a lot done by the time I went to bed.

I have to admit I did feel better and clean now. I had let myself go since the kids had come to live with me. I put on 25 lbs. which was coming off right away. I like to look neat when I was traveling so I would get a new wardrobe. Maybe have my hair styled which I hadn't done since---Wow I don't remember the last time. So it's been that long huh. First thing in the morning my life changes again. I knew the food was no good and I was now hungry so I made a run to the local market.

When I returned I was putting some of the groceries away and heard a woman's voice. I turned around and saw no one. I went to the front door and it was standing wide open. *I know I shut the door and locked it.* What's going on I wondered. When I went back into the kitchen I thought I saw a figure going down the hallway. I went into every room and saw no one. *Must be my mind playing tricks on me........*

I fell into bed that night and sleep like a weight had been lifted from my shoulders. I'm not sure why but it felt good. Maybe it was because I had finally made a decision.

The next morning I called my boss Ellen who had been patiently awaiting my call. Ellen was a very charming career woman who always dressed to kill. She looked like a million bucks all the time. I envied her now just thinking of how I had let myself go. I wondered if she would want me representing her firm now the way I looked. "Hi Ellen, it's me Amy." She said she knew I would call and when I ask her how she knew she said, "You my dear Amy are a career woman and that never changes. I have had a lot of employees through the years and I can tell."

"Well if things had gone right I wouldn't be here you do know that don't you?"

She gave a little laugh and said.. "I knew you'd be back. Are you ready to start traveling?" she asked.

"I guess so as ready as I'll ever be." I replied to her. She seemed to know me better than I knew myself. As if she had my life planned out for me.

The next day I went over the clothing line I was to look for with her and it did feel like old times. I think I did miss it. Ya maybe she did know me pretty good. I really got into it that day and the next. I was scheduled to leave for Paris in 3 days and I have to admit I was getting excited. She told me to buy some new cloths on her as she gave me a credit card.

When Monday came I was on a plane with heart in hand and was having second thoughts. I had to shake that feeling if I was going to do a good job. We landed in Paris and I saw what had attracted me to Paris the first time. The scenery and the buildings were beautiful as I watched from the cab window. I loved the charm of this great city. It was so peaceful---the friendly people---the culture. I found myself so glad to be back once again. We arrived at the hotel and once again Ellen had booked me a suite for my stay. She didn't have to tell me what to expect or what to do she knew I would do it right the first time. That's why she said she wanted me back.

CHAPTER 23

I HAD NO LONGER gotten settled in my room when I heard a knock on the door. When I answered it no one was there. I looked up and down the hallways and no one was to be seen. I figured it was a prankster having fun. I ordered room service for dinner as I was tired from the trip. I had forgotten how good the food was here. After I scarfed down way more than I should have I retired and into what I thought was going to be a restful night sleep. Oh how wrong I was. Someone kept knocking one the door all night long. I finally did called the front desk and complained. "Look I'm all for people having a good time but getting ridiculous. I need to get some sleep I have a lot of work to do tomorrow. Do you think you can find out who this is and ask them to please stop knocking on my door." I know I sounded agitated because I was.

"Yes miss, we will and we do apologize. Please rest peacefully now." The clerk at the front desk replied.

I was tired the next day but I had to do my job. I had a full schedule. After a day of meetings and looking at clothing lines and interviewing new designers I was exhausted. I stopped at the desk to ask for another pillow and the desk clerk said. "Miss we looked at all of our surveillance tapes from night last and there was absolutely no one in the hallway. We saw no one knocking on your door at all."

"Well your tapes have to be wrong because it went on most of the night til I called you." I answered.

"I'm sorry---they showed no one. The men watched them for a very long time and saw no one approach your door at all."

With that reply I said. "Your tapes are wrong," and I left. Man I don't believe this. Maybe it's someone at the hotel playing games. I don't know but I do know someone was knocking on my door....

After having a bit of dinner I retired to my room and sank into a hot bath. Bubbles and hot water, there's nothing better to sooth your aching bones. I hadn't been so active in a long time and I was feeling it from head to toe. As I lay there thinking about the day and knowing it went well. I had discovered a line of clothing Ellen was going to love. Right now--- I was loving myself for being so good. Oh I know it sounds conceded but really damn I was good at my job. The line was from a young girl fresh out of designer school but don't let that fool you she knows what she's doing. Better yet she knows what the young crowd wants.

She had designed the most amazing line of young women's clothing that I had seen in a very long time. They were all right on the mark and so classy and sassy and new. I was very pleased with myself for checking her out and contracting her line. They will all be loved in the states.

I finished my bath and climbed into bed with my work in hand. There was a rattle on the door knob. I got up and looked out the peep hole but didn't see anyone. I was going to open the door but thought what if they were still out there. So I decided to watch for a minute. I saw no one. I went back to bed and fell asleep. I was tired from no sleep the night before.

To my surprise I woke refreshed the next morning and headed off to work. As I stopped in a little café for coffee I noticed a very good looking gentleman watching me. I was flattered but not even ready to meet a guy. He was impressive very clean cut with a very expensive suit on. What he was doing in this little café was beyond me. I noticed he watched me all the way out the café and down the street. *Ya well that's not going to happen any time soon.*

My day went as usual and very quickly. I was starving because I missed lunch. I was working with a photographer and we wanted to get the line shot so I could fax it to Ellen. I stopped at the cafe for dinner and guess who was there. Yes you guess it the nice looking gentleman from this morning. He saw me come in and immediately came to my table and asked if he could join me. "I'm sorry do I know you?" I asked.

"I am Phillip Meanger. I live over on Steel Street I own Meanger bank and Trust just down the street. I am not married and do not have a girl friend so please may I meet you?"

As I laughed I said, "I'm sorry I love your accent. It's refreshing and I must say you are very polite."

"I say thank you now? Is right?" while he stumbled with his words.

"Yes, is right Phillip." I couldn't help but smile he was funny the way he was trying to impress me. I asked him to sit and he smiled a beautiful smile. Very nice looking man I thought. He probably has a lot of women after him. So why me?

What could it hurt to have some company while in a country that I don't know anyone? So we sat and chatted--- ate dinner and to my surprise it was pleasant enough. He looked over at me with the most delicious eyes and said he wanted me to be his wife. Woo hold on hear this was totally unexpected. "I live in a big you call mansion and have enough money that you no have to work anymore." Needless to say I was speechless. "Look...it was very nice having dinner with you and I would like to do it again but I'm not looking to get married or even have a boyfriend. Sorry."

"No it is I who is sorry it was like you say too quickly. We meet here tomorrow night for dinner yes?"

"Ok we can have dinner again I would like that, but---now I have to go it's getting late and I have a early morning appointment."

"Very nice to have dinner with you." He said as I got up to leave.

"Very nice to have dinner with you too." I smiled as I left the café.

Wow what just happened. I was very flattered but not ready for marriage.

I laughed all the way back to the hotel. What a trip I thought I came back here to do work and get a marriage proposal. He lives in a mansion huh.

Maybe I should check this out. LOL

CHAPTER 24

THERE WAS A NOTE on my door when I arrived. I grabbed it and went inside. It was extremely nice handwriting and as I opened it I could smell perfume I think. I read the words and couldn't believe it. I stared at the paper and waited for the words to change but they didn't. *What the hell is going on.* It said,

If I was you I wouldn't go to work tomorrow something bad will happen to you...

It wasn't signed and I had no idea what they were talking about. I didn't know what to think so I went down to the clerk and showed him the note and asked him to look at the surveillance camera to see who left the note on my door. He went to the back room and as I waited for him I couldn't imagine who would have sent me a note like this.

"Miss Grant I don't know what to tell you but we went through the tape on fast forward and absolutely no one was at your door all day."

"Someone had to put it there."

"I'm sorry but no one was there all day you can come watch the tape if you like."

"No that's ok I believe you but how did it get there? I don't understand."

"I don't know. Are you ok Miss Grant?" The clerk asked with concern in his voice.

"Ya, Ya---I'm Ok. Thanks goodnight." I rudely replied as I left for my room.

The next morning I was ready early for my appointment so I stopped at the café for coffee and noticed a young boy sitting on the curb crying. I said, "Is something wrong, can I help you?" He looked up at me with red swollen eyes and said. "No I'm just hungry and have no money and nowhere to live. My Momma & Papa are both dead and I roam the streets all day trying to find some food and shelter for the night."

"How old are you."

"I'm 11 but I look older and I know how to take care of myself." He added very quickly.

"I'm sure you do and I'm sorry but I think you do look 11. Can I buy you breakfast?"

"You would do that for me? You don't even know me."

"Yes come with me---I would do that for you." As we entered the café I found a table and sat him down. I told him to order anything on the menu. He smiled up at me and that was thanks enough.

I asked the waitress to bring him anything he wanted until he couldn't eat anymore. She said. "Are you sure Miss?" "Sometimes these kids can eat a whole lot."

"Fill him up and with that I left $40.00 to feed him."

"Thank you lady!" he said with a big smile on his face. I just couldn't believe he was so alone at the age of 11. I asked waitress. "Don't you have shelters these kids can go to? Or Maybe there's a home for orphan kids?"

"No we have nothing like that the kids run the streets all day long some of them at night."

"Wow I had no idea it was so bad. I have to go please just feed him please." She said she would and I headed off to work.

When I got to my appointment I saw very nervous lady walking the floor almost like pacing. She went back and forth mumbling something I couldn't make out. I think I startled her when I walked up. She looked at me and her eyes went wide open as if she had seen a ghost. She was an older lady with bleach blond hair all of her roots were dark and looked like they had not been done in a very long time. Her clothes were wrinkled and dirty. Her makeup well there wasn't any other than mascara that looked like it had been on way too long and was smeared. I wondered what she was doing here. She just didn't seem to fit.

When I told the receptionist who I was she apologized for not recognizing me from my last trip some time ago.

"That's ok I've been a little out of commission

but I'm back now and ready to go. Are they ready for me?"

"Sure are, go on in."

We were discussing and ad campaign that would help everyone when all of a sudden I heard someone screaming. It turned out to be the lady in the waiting room who I had seen when I came in. She was screaming bloody murder. We all went to the door and she was running around in circles---pulling at her hair. The receptionist said she had called the police and they were on their way. Mr. Scovel said to take care of it and we went back in the room. There was a large window between the room we were in and the waiting room. It had blinds that were pulled closed. We couldn't see what she was doing but believe me we could hear her.

I don't know what happened but the window came crashing in and glass flew everywhere with the lady from the waiting room landing right on top of me. She was all bloody and heavy. I couldn't move. She had me pinned down. Mr. Scovel grabbed at her to remove her and I was covered in blood. He gently laid her on the floor and checked for a pulse. He looked up at me and said, "I think she's dead."

"Oh my God, are you sure?" I asked.

"I don't feel a pulse at all but we'll wait til the police get here. Come on let's move to another room." With that we all went around the corner to another room to wait for the police. She looked so bad I didn't know what had just happened.

I found out later the lady was hooked on prescription drugs and was having withdrawals. She couldn't afford the drugs anymore and was actually the wife of one of the men who worked there. He was out in the field when she came in. He was headed back to the office now. The police showed up first then the paramedics finally the coroner. The husband came in after they had taken her away but didn't seem very upset at all. As a matter of fact he was joking with one of the other guys there. How rude I thought your wife just dies and you're out here joking around. What a jerk I wanted to tell him where to go. I gave him a disgusting look and he decided to leave the room. That was ok with me.

I wondered if this was what the note I

had received was talking about....I don't know I just wanted to get out of here and forget all about it.

I told Mr. Scovel I was leaving. "OK Amy I understand it's been one crazy day. I'll call Ellen and finish up with the details. You go on I'll take care of yourself." He smiled at me and gave me a hug and '*no it didn't make me feel better*' but I had to get out of there.

On the way home I saw a bus full of kids coming home from school. My thought immediately went to Shelly and Jason. I wondered if they were ok and if they liked their new schools. I knew Sammy would be visiting them but I just couldn't bring myself to more heartache. So I decided to stay away from the completely.

CHAPTER 25

WHEN I GOT BACK to the hotel the phone was blinking I had a message. I called the front desk and they said Phillip had called and wanted to know when I would be ready for dinner. I remembered we hadn't set a time. They gave me his number so I called and was going to back out after today but he answered and it sounded like familiar voice and I told him I would be ready at 6:30. He said he would be out front waiting for me. It was early so I showered and took my time doing my hair and makeup. I needed the peace and quiet. As time got closer I decided to go down to the bar and have a drink while I waited.

There was a guy playing smooth sounds on a piano. It was refreshing and very enjoyable. I was humming and watching the piano player when I noticed it was time to meet Phillip. I walked out the front door and saw this big beautiful white carriage with Phillip standing next to it. "Your ride awaits madam."

"Are you serious? It's gorgeous. I can't believe you're taking me on a carriage ride." I couldn't help it I was laughing.

"A--- What kind of ride?"

"Carriage---what do they call it here? We call it a carriage." I said.

"It is called a rolling cart. Very, how you say popular." He was stumbling with his words. I loved the way he talked.

"Well it is a very beautiful rolling cart and it was very nice of you to do this. Thank you Phillip."

He helped me into the *'rolling cart'* and we took off into the wild unknown. "I thought we could ride a bit I wanted to talk to you. I know you are new here and I am not but I think we are good together yes?"

" Ya, I think we get along pretty good but we haven't know each other very long." I answered. "Yes, but I do think I love you. No I am sure. I wanted to do this proper so (*as he got down on one knee in the rolling cart*) Lady Amy will you please be married to me?"

OMG I thought was he serious? He pulled out a box and opened it and my heart sank and mouth went open it had to be a 4 carat diamond ring. The biggest stone I had ever seen. I thought the carriage was beautiful wow this was unbelievable and so big too. I was speechless I really couldn't speak. I opened my mouth but the words wouldn't come out. Holy S*&^#. I said. "Give me a minute Phillip I don't know what to say."

"First, before you answer I have to show you something." He got back in the seat and said. "Don't answer now I have to show you." I hadn't noticed how far we had driven but I saw lights up a ways and assumed that's where we were going for dinner.

We rode the rest of the way in silence. I was glad because I still didn't know what to say. We pulled up in front of this huge mansion.

Oh I bet this is where he lives.

"Please come I want to show you." He helped me out of the carriage and led me in through two tall maybe 10' doors. They looked hand carved stunning. I was shocked at the décor inside it was unbelievable again...

"This is where we dine and you look around and see where you will live. You do nothing there is someone to do everything for you all the time." Boy did that sound good to good to be true. I saw so many chandeliers, marble everywhere, antiques, paintings, statues, wow my head was spinning. He lead me to the dining room and just a s the entry was fabulous. I can't think of enough words to describe this place. Yes defiantly a mansion.

We sat and ate the most delicious food. I don't know I lost count 7-8-9 course meal. "Phillip I think this is all wonderful but I didn't come to Paris to meet a guy or get married. I came to get away from that kind of life and go back to my career." "Shh." he said "I don't need an answer now. You will be here another 3 days please think about it and let me know then. OK?"

"Ok, we really do get along pretty good don't

we?" I laughed as I think the wine was getting to me. We had a few more glasses and he took me home like a gentleman. The next three days I didn't have a lot to do since I had made the deal and found the line right away. So I thought I would give him a chance. I mean come on if you could have seen this place.

We made a date to go riding tomorrow but not in a rolling cart on bicycles of all things. Phillip said we could really see the country side this way. So I figured if this guy who was worth what looked like millions could ride a bike I could too.

The bikes were kind of scary at first I hadn't been on a bike since I was a kid. I did get used to it and it all came back how to ride. I didn't want to look stupid or awkward riding so I tried to lag behind. Naturally Phillip kept looking back to see if I was still there. It was a bit embarrassing. But before you knew it I was riding like a champ.

The country side was awesome. The houses the scenery was great. We rode for about 4 hours and stopped in between for lunch at a cute little country house. It was charming and good food. I had a wonderful time and we got along great. It was like we had known each other for a long time and we in sync with one another. I had a great time and didn't want it to end. I think I was becoming fond of Phillip. He sure was growing on me anyway. He was a charming and quit intelligent man. I found myself looking forward to dinner with him. His house or mine although his was defiantly better. LOL

We went by this old house on the trip home and Phillip wanted to stop. "I want to say hi to someone who lives here, is it Ok with you?"

"Of course go ahead."

"No you come with me she is very sweet old lady who has been here a long time."

"Sure ok." We dismounted the bikes and leaned them up against the fence. He opened the gate for me and I could smell something wonderful coming from inside the cottage. Phillip knocked on the door and this sweet looking old lady came to the door and started saying

"Phillip, Phillip come in please come in. I'm so glad to see you." She looked over at me and said, "you have brought a friend I see." Then she chuckled and said almost in a laughing whisper. "Ooh she is quite pretty you naughty boy. I knew one day you would settle down and I do believe this one may be the right one for you. You're not getting any younger you know."

He hugged her and said, "Ok that's enough your making me red in the face." He laughed along with her. "Amy this is Sophie she runs these parts around here."

I was laughing at them both they were defiantly funny. After chatting with her for a while and she showed me around her home including all the animals she had we started back to the hotel. I was glad to be getting off the bike though because my backside was feeling that skinny unpadded seat.

CHAPTER 26

PHILLIP WANTED TO dine at his house--- scratch that--- mansion again so I agreed. This mansion was so big and the décor was like something out of the past. He has large like King Louie chairs, huge glass hutches--- they had to be 8-9 foot long full of what looked like very expensive china and figurines. There were swords with gold blades lining the walls going up the most elegant staircase. I thought the house back in Oregon was nice this place was a true elegant mansion. It was nice there and the food like I said was to die for.

We ate and he took me into this room that was dark. After turning the lights on I could see it was a theater, a very large theater like the ones you go to back home and pay $20.00 a person to see a movie. The seats were all theater style recliners and there must have been 75-100, with a screen as large as the whole front of my house. The floors were all done in a beautiful caramel colored marble with dark veins running through it. This house was quite magnificent. The chairs you just sank into and wanted to fall asleep. He poured me a glass of wine and sat down next to me. He had a remote and turned on a comity show *a Paris comedy show*. Although I didn't quite understand it there were parts that did make me laugh. He seemed quite humored that I thought it was funny.

When it was over I said, "Phillip I should get back to the hotel I have some work I have to catch up on. You've been keeping me so busy but I really do have to have it done before I go back to the states." He got quiet all of a sudden and I thought I had said something wrong.

"You are going back?"

"Yes, I have to I was only to be here for two weeks. My company needs me to be there when the new shipment arrives."

He reached over and said, "I don't want you to go. I want you here with me forever." Then he leaned in and kissed me with a long lingering kiss which did absolutely nothing for me. No fireworks, no sparklers nothing. This was not good with everything he had to offer me and no fireworks. That sucks. I mean really I didn't feel anything at all but wet lips.

I smiled and said I really had to go. He got up and said he would drive me back. I got my coat and we headed back to the hotel. I got out and as he was driving away I put my hands in my pockets and felt a box. Oh, great he had put that huge diamond ring in my pocket. I guess for me to look at and think about it. Boy have I been thinking about it. I wonder how it would work if I did marry him even though there were no fireworks.

Could we get along good enough to overcome the fireworks that hadn't been there? With everything Phillip has to offer I'd love to give it a shot. But I don't know. I would have to move to Paris, have a huge ring, and live in a

huge, huge mansion, maids
to do all the work. Boy you would think that would be a no brainer. I need to sleep on this one.

The last few years have been so screwed up. I lay in bed for what seemed like hours wondering what it would be like. I thought about the life I thought I had back home. The life I had that fell apart. I thought about the kids and Sammy. I could never forget about that life. But I could start over again. I could go home and clean up what I had to and I think Ellen wouldn't like it but I could make it work. So I decided to tell Phillip I would marry him and move here to his mansion. With that decision being made
I feel asleep.

Phillip met me the next morning for breakfast at the café and I told him.
"Phillip I want to tell you something." He had a sad look on his face. "I know we haven't known each other very long. When you kissed me last night there were no fireworks." He had a puzzled look on his face so I explained what the fireworks meant to me.
"So because I didn't feel fireworks I don't think

I love you but before I answer you please, listen---to what I have to say. Ok"

"Yes that works for me fine because I do love you and I know in time you will love me too. So you really will marry me?" "Phillip we just met how can you say you love me so soon. You don't even know me."

"Amy a person just knows and I know."

"I have to tell you why I'm here. There was at a car wreck in front of my house a few years back and I made a promise to a woman who was dying." I proceeded to tell him all about the long story and crazy things I had been through. When I finished telling him he looked at me and said. "Amy I can take all the pain away. You will never have to worry about any of it again. I will keep you busy and in time I know you will love me."

"My story doesn't bother you? Or to know that I still love another man doesn't bother you? You, could marry me knowing that?"

"Yes I would marry you now if you would have me."

I looked into his face and saw the determination in his eyes. He was serious. I put my hands on his face and said. "Then yes I will marry you

Phillip Meanger."

He grabbed me and kissed me very tenderly and smiled softly. Oh yes I think I see the fireworks you talk about. Enough for both of us yes" Then he looked up at the sky and let out a yell. It was a very loud yelling but never the less it was a happy yell.

We talked for a long time planning the wedding and the honeymoon. He wanted to have a pre wedding party and invite all his friends, relatives and associates. He said he wanted to fly my friends and relatives over too. He wanted to get married as soon as possible. I was like--- in a daze it was happening so fast. He told me he wanted me to invite my relatives and friends from the states. I told him I didn't have a family but he said he would fly everyone over in his jet. *Jet did he say his jet? He owned a jet? Wow.*

He had me call my friends the next morning and set up for them to be picked up in 2 weeks. Everyone agreed. I only had about 7 friends that I knew well enough to invite. That was enough I had a feeling he would make up for it with his friends.

I talked to Ellen she was leery and keep

saying you just met him are you crazy? I told
her yes I probably was but I was doing this.
"What about Sammy?" She asked.
"Oh I think Sammy and I are done for good."
"But you still love him don't you?"
"You know I do but I can't wait on him I
have to live my life while I can. Besides
remember he's the one who walked out on me."
I said.
"Ya I remember but you two were made for
each other and what about the kids?"
"I can't handle seeing them once in a while---
we are all better off---look this is the way it
is ok?" I told her I didn't want to talk about
it anymore. So she was going to get
everyone together and plan the trip. "I have
to admit Ellen I am getting excited."
"Let me know when and where and we will
see you in a couple of weeks. You are
sure Amy?"
"Yes Ellen I am sure. I'll see you soon. Be
happy for me." Well that was done and now for
the planning of the *wedding.*

CHAPTER 27

THE PLANNING WAS crazy. Phillip had hired a lady to help me and she was very nice and courteous. Her name was Martha. She knew exactly what to do she told me she had planned many parties for Phillip. He told her he was very pleased with her work. She showed me a sketch of what the hall would look like. She seemed to know what Phillip wanted without him telling her. The setting was beautiful and the tables many, many of them were elegantly decorated. I told her it looked like something fit for a King. She turned to me and smiled.

Martha was in the kitchen one day and I overheard her saying she liked me better than the others because she felt I was honest and not after Phillips money. *Others, what others I wondered how many she was talking about. Phillips money I was comfortable I didn't need his money.* I guess I would have to talk to her and find out about the 'others.'

When I called Catherine (my acquaintance from work) she was so happy and suggested if I got board I could always work from here. I sent her a picture of me and Philip after her insisting. She called to say. "You look so happy and Phillip is very good looking and rich too--- what a combination." she said. "Some girls have all the luck." I didn't say anything and she added. "I'm sorry Amy I didn't mean it that way."

"It's ok Catherine that part of my life I guess is over. I'm moving on. And yes he is handsome." "I can't wait to see you and that mansion he lives in. That mansion you will be living in too. I'll call you in a couple of days to get the exact time to be at the airport. Bye, bye get the time to be at the airort. Bye,bye, I'll see you soon." "Bye Catherine, be safe we'll see you when you get here."

The next day was busy Martha had a million questions for me. How did I want this and how did I want that. She kept me hopping. I finally got her alone and told her I had overheard what she was saying to the others and wanted to know what she meant about and how many others were there.

"I'm sorry I didn't mean for you to hear me. I would hate it if Mr. Phillip knew I was overheard. He'll fire me."

"Don't worry I'm not going to tell him, but I am going to ask him how many girls he has gone with. I won't mention you."

"Thank you Miss Amy."

I decide to wait until we were alone tonight to ask him. He would be relaxed and I did want to know. After we had dinner we retired to the sitting room. I had told Phillip I wanted to talk to him.

"Phillip will you answer a couple of questions for me?"

"Yes, what is it?" he said.

"I was wondering how many other women you

have been with. Like seriously or seeing for a while." At that point I felt really stupid asking him after I had told him I was still in love with another man.

"Well, let see I guess about 500 or more." He said smiling.

"I'm serious how many?"

"Does it really matter to you that much?" He said as he leaned over, and kissed me.

"Yes I'd like an answer." I kind of pulled back so he would answer me.

"I have been with a few but never anyone like you. I never felt like I do when I'm with you. Does that answer your question?"

"Is that as good as you can do?" He looked a little puzzled and I added. " You're not going to give me a straight answer are you?"

"No I'm not. I don't think it's important. You're the one I'm with and you're the one I have asked to marry me. Isn't that good enough?"

"I guess it'll have to be for now." So I asked him to take me back to the hotel which he did. I told him I would see him the next day.

I soaked in a hot tub after such a filled day of choices. It had been hectic. All day there was people running around. I just wanted to bath and fall into bed. I started to read a book when I heard something in the bathroom. As I got up the light went on. Scared yea I think so. I froze in my tracks. I hadn't had any trouble for a while and this was really freaking me out. I wanted to know who it was but I was afraid to go in there. I edged my way to the door and realized I didn't have my robe on. *Do I go back for it or get out of there?* I decided to go so I gently reached for the door handle---unlocked the door and slowly opened it.

When I thought it was clear I ran down the hallway as fast as I could. I flew down the stairs as the elevator wasn't open. When I reached the lobby thank God there wasn't anyone there except the lady behind the counter. I was out of breath when I reached her and told about the noise and light coming on in the bathroom. She assured me she would send someone up there right away. "Thank you it really scared me. Do you have a blanket I can wrap in?" I asked her.

"Sure let me get one." She replied.

She returned with a warm blanket for me and I realized I was shivering. The desk clerk helped me to a chair in the lobby where I waited on pins and needles until the security came down.

"Miss Grant?" He said.

"Yes?" While still shaking I replied.

"We went through your room from top to bottom and no one is there. If someone was in your room you can rest assured they are gone now. "

"What do you mean *'If someone was there, who would have turned the light on?"*

"I'm sorry miss but the light was off and door was open." He said.

"Well then they left after I did because the light was on when I came down here and the door was shut." I said angrily. I ask if they could give me another room for the night and help me with my bags and they did. After I moved rooms I didn't see or hear anything else all night. *'That was just fine with me.'*

CHAPTER 28

WITH EVERYTHING THAT was going on with the reception I completely forgot that Phillip was taking me to lunch tomorrow and he told me to wear something nice. So I pulled out the old checkbook and went shopping. I stopped in this cute little dress shop in the village and found the most amazing dress. I ask who the designer was and the young lady said. "I am why, is there something wrong with it?" "No not at all it is extremely nice and very well made. I love the way it flows and the colors are very well chosen. I'm Amy Grant what's your name?"

"I'm Sally Waldon nice to meet you. You seem to know a lot about clothing are you a designer too?" She asked.

"NO, no, I'm the one who buys clothing lines and make young ladies like you very famous and rich. (Her eyes were wide open by now and mouth open as well.) Are you interested?" I replied smiling because of the find I just made. "May I see some of your other designs?"

"Oh yes you certainly may. Come with me." She said while grinning back from ear to ear. She turned around and said "Are you for real this isn't a joke---is it?"

"No joke sweetie, show me your line of clothing." She was very young but very talented. If her other clothing was a nice as this dress it will be a great find.

I went through her line and was amazed at the designs and colors. She truly was talented. I had to have her line so I made her an offer she couldn't refuse. I knew Ellen would be profoundly happy.

I had to hurry now to meet Phillip for our lunch date. I rushed back to the hotel and showered and changed I looked stunning in this dress. I was pleased with myself for finding this young lady.

I met Phillip, he said I looked ravishing. "Thank you Phillip that's nice of you to say." I answered as we got into the long limo. We hadn't driven very far when we turned, onto a road that leads to the airport. I looked out the tinted window and saw this beautiful jet sitting beside us as we came to a stop. "Is this one of your jets Phillip?"

"Yes it and about 12 others over there along the runway." He replied.

"OMG are you serious?"

"Yes my dear I am serious. Are you ready for your trip for lunch? By the way why do you say OMG?"

"It's just a shortcut to saying "Oh My God" and Yes I'm ready. Where are we going?"

"We are having lunch in a small but very rich town. They have the most amazing food. I wanted you to taste it and see the wealth in this tiny town. It's so small it doesn't even have a name."

"Sounds great how far away is it?" I ask because I wanted to call Ellen and tell her about my find.

"Oh it's a 35 min by plane. This by the way is the only way you can get to it. It's a small island of the coast. It won't take long."

When the plane took off I was shocked at the way it seemed to go straight up at once. It was really smooth and quite. We settled into our seats and were served a glass of wine. "I swear Phillip I think you are always trying to get me drunk."

"Not at all, I just thought you liked wine. I didn't mean to..." "That's ok I'm just kidding." I interrupted. He smiled but didn't seem to be happy with my kidding. I think he was offended. "I'm sorry I didn't mean to make you mad.'

"I'm not mad." He said. "I just don't want you to think I'm trying to take advantage of you."

"I'm the one who's sorry Phillip I forget your customs and mine are different. I didn't mean to offend you at all."

We rode in silence the rest of the way and it was somewhat awkward. I kept myself occupied by looking out the window at the water below. We weren't flying very high and I could see the ocean now. It was a peaceful blue/green with some whitecaps.

When we arrived I apologized again and Phillip seemed to forgive me. We exited the plane and yet another limo was there to pick us up. I think I have to be careful as to what I say to Phillip he gets upset when I make jokes or kid him.

We approached a very old looking building. It seemed to be popular as there were a good number of people waiting outside to get in. The door to the limo opened---the people started moving around then there was a round of cheering like I hadn't heard before. It was so close. We had a hard time getting into the restaurant because of so many people wanting Phillip to stop and talk to them. I came to realize he was a very popular man in this town. He was right the food was probably the best food I had ever eaten. I thanked him for taking me to such a special place. He smiled and knew he did well.

On the trip home I told him about the designer I had found in town and told him she made the dress I had on. He became quite mad and said I wasn't to talk to her again. I was shocked--- what was wrong with him. I didn't understand why he was so mad. Again the trip back was very quiet and rather awkward

When we got back to the mansion I told him I wanted to return to my hotel. He told his driver to take me back and then just walked inside without saying another word.

I'm thinking what did I say to make him so mad? I know he was pretty mad and I need to ask some question about this girl and see what the problem was.

I guess you could say we had our first fight. Didn't take long we haven't known each other long at all. Afternoon turned into evening and I hadn't heard from Phillip at all. I wasn't going to call him because I didn't think I did anything wrong. He needs to apologize to me this time.

I don't know--- was this all wrong? Was I fooling myself? Could I really be happy with Phillip? He had swept me off my feet---maybe I was just caught up in the romance since the bad scene in Oregon with Sammy and the kids--- court---custody, the whole mess.

Well another night of soul searching. I wasn't going to sleep good tonight either. I wanted to go over everything in my head again and see if this will really work. I've been on my own for so long and just not sure if I want to take on the whole wild dream I was being handed on a silver (no---gold) platter. All my life I thought I was settled and secure with everything I needed until I met Sammy. That changed my whole life. Now that it was over with him and I was being offered all the things Phillip could give me, why would I turn it down.

CHAPTER 29

I TOSSED AND turned all night again and still couldn't come up with a reason why I shouldn't marry Phillip.

The phone rang and snapped me out of my conversation I was having with myself. It was Martha calling to tell me the limo would be here to pick me up at 8:00 sharp.

"We have so much to do Miss Amy or we'll never be ready for the party and wedding."

"Have you talked to Phillip this morning?" I asked.

"Yes he agrees we have to get busy and finish

time is---how you say speeding."

I chuckled and said, "flying Martha time is flying."

"Yes---Yes that it is I forget. So please be ready. OK?"

"OK---I'll be ready when it gets here. I'll see you in a bit." I said as I hung up the phone.

When the limo arrived I was ready for the planning but first to talk to Phillip about his behavior last night. I wanted to know why he got so mad. When the limo arrived the driver opened the door for me---I went to get in and saw Phillip was in the limo. He smiled and said "I'm sorry Amy--- it's just some things you don't know about me."

"Well were going to get married and don't you think I should know some things about you?" letting him know I was still a little irritated.

"I had a problem with this girl and it was a bad taste in my mouth. I should have told you but I didn't know you would meet her."

"Phillip---*I said smiling*---if you just tell me things that you think you should---then I won't be surprised when I meet people you have had a---bad taste in your mouth about." Where I come from honesty is very important in a marriage.

He looked at me smiling too so I assumed everything was ok.

"I will tell you but just not right now---is that ok with you?"

"That's fine so let's get to planning this party and wedding." He leaned over and kissed me and we rode the rest of the way talking about the plans. He was in charge since it was his house and money. I felt he liked being in charge---so I let him be.

We got to the mansion and Phillip went his way and I headed to find Martha. It was a full day of choosing flowers---food---colors---I sampled so much food I was stuffed by dinner time. More times than not I would pick something out and Martha would say. "Oh dear I don't think Sir Phillip would like that. Maybe choose this one." So I chose the one Martha had suggested. Like I said it was his money paying for the wedding.

I was exhausted so Phillip suggested I stay there and he would send someone for cloths and I would be refreshed in the morning. So I was led to one of the 15 bedrooms in the mansion and it was beautiful. The bed was a four poster with this huge headboard---done in a mahogany I think. There was a table and chairs and lounge a game table Wow this was a whole house in this one room. Martha got me set up with a gown ran my bath water. And then she even popped down to the kitchen and had some cocoa made for me right after my bath.

"Boy---I could really get used to this. The bath was heavenly and by the way thank you so much for the cocoa."

"You are welcome Miss Amy. I will see you in the morning about 8:00 is that ok?"

"That will be fine I will see you downstairs."

I fell into bed and I mean '*fell into bed*' it was so soft and fluffy. I sank halfway down but it was very comfy. I must have fallen asleep right away and before I knew---it I could see light coming in the window. I looked at the clock on the nightstand '*the nightstand was as big as my dresser.*' "Wow" 7:30 I jumped out of bed and rushed to get dressed. OWE I screamed as I hit my big toe on the corner bedpost. "Mm —Mm—Mm…." After grabbing my toe I was almost crying it hurt so much. I sat there for a few minutes feeling sorry for my big toe and finally finished getting ready and headed down stairs to meet Phillip for breakfast all the time thinking boy am I going to put on the pounds. LOL

The day went by slowly and I was so confused with all the preparations. The custom here was so different than ours--- I knew this but some of the things they did were downright strange.   Martha said. "We have to put the flowers in vinegar for one day before the wedding because it purifies them."

"What---put them in vinegar are you sure?" I asked.

"She turned and looked at me a said. "Of course you do want your marriage to last don't you?"

"Well yes---but vinegar?" I laughed because it sounded so crazy. I have never heard of this before in any country. "I'm sorry I just haven't ever heard of such a thing before--- I would think the vinegar would hurt the flower."

"Oh no it purifies them."

"I know that's what you said, I'm just having a hard time understanding it. Sorry" I said while still laughing.

Phillip showed up about that time and wanted to know what was so funny. I told him wanted to know what was so funny. I told him I was having a hard time getting used to their custom.

"I thought you had been here many times."

"Yes I have but never to get married and see the customs that are so different from ours. I'm going to have to read a book and catch up on all of your customs." I said snickering a little. "Don't worry they will come to you after you've been here a while. Come with me I want to show you something."

He took my arm and led me into the mansion. We went into his study and he handed me a stack of papers.

"What's this?" I asked.

"It's my new will. I wanted you to see it."

"Look Phillip I will sign a prenuptial---that's not a problem. I'm not marrying you for your money I have plenty of my own. Really just tell me where to sign the prenup."

"No you don't understand I have changed my will and left everything to you."

"What---no you can't--- what about your family? You can't do that. I don't want you to do that."

He replied. "I have to if something happens to me you will be next to the throne."

"You've got to be kidding---a throne what are you talking about Phillip I wouldn't even know what to do." What throne?

"I am King and you will be Queen very soon." He answered smiling.

"Wow, wait a minute you never said anything about King and Queen. No---No, I can't do this. I can't be a Queen married to a King. I can't do this I don't know what to say." I turned around and hit him in the shoulder 3-4 maybe 5 times and was screaming I'm not Queen--- I--- you didn't tell me, why didn't you tell me?" The tears started to come, I couldn't think, as I yelled back at him.

He grabbed me and pulled me close to him and said in a low voice, "Amy I'm sorry I thought you knew. Everyone knows I am King."

"Ya well not me, you could have told me while you were sweeping me off my feet. I mean *REALLY* Phillip. That's something you tell your future wife, don't cha think?"

"Please don't worry there will always be someone to help and lead you. Don't worry now I plan on living a long life." He said as he chuckled.

"You have to? Cause I'm spending the rest of my life being mad at you for this."

"Yes my soon to be wife I have to---so be happy with it."

"Ok---but I'm still not comfortable with it."

"Maybe that's why I fell in love with you so fast. You are so honest." He leaned over and kissed me on the forehead.

The rest of the day was a blur as we went through the wedding plans. I just couldn't believe Phillip didn't tell me or, that I was so stupid to not know. I couldn't imagine him not wanting to leave everything to his family. Even though he hadn't talked much about any of then. He said one time they weren't close at all.

By the time I was ready I had already had three calls up to my room to see if I was coming down. I had to take a rest in the afternoon it was all so much to take in. The chatter the buzzing the people.

CHAPTER 30

I HAD TO FIND out about Sally the designer and I figured this was as good a time as any. So I just blurted it out. "Phillip I need to know about Sally the designer. My boss Ellen really wants the clothing line and I wouldn't be dealing with her. Just to get her set up---then I wouldn't see her again. But I have to know why you got so mad at me the other day."He poured himself a glass of wine and offered me one but it was too early in the day for me to drink.

"There was an incident that I'm not very proud of and I don't want you to think I was wrong. I took her to dinner one night and things kinda got carried away. She led me on and them didn't want to go any farther but I didn't want to stop. I guess I forced her to have sex and she called the police after I left. There was a big scandal and that was unacceptable. I didn't mean to hurt her but she told the police I took advantage of her."He must have seen the concern on my face because he kept apologizing to me.

"You don't have to apologize to me, b ut I do want to make it clear and I want your promise that it will never happen to me. If I tell you NO I mean no. Is that clear?"

"Oh yes I understand and it was a onetime thing I just misunderstood her, b ut I didn't want her to tell you---I wanted to explain it to you myself."

"Ok as long as were clear on that. So what happened?"

"I was arrested and put into house jail for 2 days until I told her I was sorry and gave her money to open her store."

"Really how much did you give her?"

"That's not important."

"Yes it is to me---it will tell me what kind of

person I am dealing with."

"I ended up giving her over $50,000.00."

"Wow that's a lot. Ok, well it's all over right."

"It's all over at last." He said with a sigh of relief. "I just wanted to tell you."

"I wanted to tell you something too. Do you remember the day I came out here and you asked me why I seemed so preoccupied?"

"Yes I remember. I knew something had happened."

"Well I have had a lot of phone calls and no one is on the other end. Then one night I heard a noise in the bathroom---the light was turned on and the door was shut. I never leave the light on and I always leave the door open. When the security went to my room they didn't find anything but the light was off and the door open. I know someone was in there. That's why they changed my room. I wouldn't stay in that room any longer. Well I started hearing noises and I'm getting phone calls again but no one's on the other line."

"We will get your things and you will stay here."

"That's not why I'm telling you this. I thought I saw a shadow two nights ago. It looked like the lady I helped in the accident. I know it's not possible but I think it might be her ghost. I don't know why she is here. I haven't said anything to anyone til now. I don't know what to do about it."

"Look we are moving you today I don't want you scared or you might get wrinkles before the wedding."

I must have really had a weird look on my face because he said. "I just make a joke right it was funny me kidding." He was trying to be funny. Funny was not what Phillip was he was very bad at trying to make you laugh. He was so bad that he actually did make me laugh at his trying. I'm sure he thought he was being funny.

He called the Limo to pick us up and we went to move me out at his insistence. I just wanted to tell someone what was happening--- or what I thought was happening. When we got to the hotel he told the clerk he was taking me to his place and the clerk assured him they hadn't found anything even though they had looked and looked.

"We will be leaving as soon as Miss Amy is ready."

"Phillip it wasn't their fault---don't be mad at them. This has to do with me. I'm thinking maybe I just have the wedding jitters. I'm nervous you know?"

"Ok get your stuff together and Arthur will take it to the limo."

When I was almost packed up to go I turned to make a sweep around the room to see if I had gotten everything and a shadow again ran into the bathroom. '*Boy I'm actually glad to get out of here.*' I called Arthur who was standing outside my door---he started getting my things and I headed out as fast as I could.

"Very sorry to see you go miss."

"Thank you---will you please forward any mail that comes to Phillip's."

"Yes we will it was a pleasure to have you here. Please come again." "Goodbye."

As we walked out the door we ran smack dab into Sally. Needless to say we were all a bit shocked. She gave Phillip a quick look and said hi to me and hurried down the street. She seemed a bit shaken up as she scurried away. I needed to talk to her and see if we could work together through Ellen at work. I didn't know how to go about it without Phillip getting mad again.

When we returned to the mansion Phillip said he wanted to discuss our honeymoon. I followed him to the limo and we took a ride. He said."I want our honeymoon to be special and wondered if you would be ok with going on my boat for a couple of weeks. We could sail as far and see as much as you wanted."

"That sounds great---I'd love to do that. We could get to know each other some more and spend some time together."

"The one thing is my boat—(as he showed me a picture of this 300ft long *'boat'*) is in Florida. We would have to go there to go out to sea. Would that be ok with you?"

"Sure that would be fine *'still stunned by the 300ft 'boat'* anywhere you want to go will be fine with me. I haven't been on a *'boat'* that big before. I would love it."

"Ok it's settled we ship off to unknown." He said while smiling.

"I have something else I want to show you come with me." He took my hand and led me to another room. "Close your eyes." He said----as he opened the door and led me in.

"I want to know what you think of this now

open your eyes."

I was shocked and flabbergasted at the most gorgeous wedding dress I had ever seen. It was so big and full with a Train as long as a football field. I didn't know what to say and had tears in my eyes. He wanted me to try it on but as I protested and explained why he said OK. "Phillip it is beautiful. But you're not supposed to see the dress before the wedding." "That's your custom not mine. We have to make sure the dress fits the bride. So Martha will help you try it on and you can model it for me. Ok?"

"Yes ok I'd love to try it on." I looked at the size and it was right. "How did you know my size?"

"Martha looked at your dresses and told me what size. She is very good with numbers."

With some help from Martha I put the dress on and felt like a Queen. It was exquisite. A bit heavy but I figured I wouldn't be doing the funky chicken at our wedding. I didn't even know if Phillip could dance. I'd love to dance on my wedding day.

Martha called Phillip (*who won the opportunity to see me in my dress*) when I was ready and he came in with a very large grin on his face---he was walking around me looking at every angle he finally said. "You are the most beautiful bride I have ever seen. I am so lucky to have you. Will you marry me?"

As I laughed I said, "You already asked me remember? It will take me another hour to get out of it. But I just love it. It's perfect Phillip just perfect. Can I sleep in it?"

He chuckled and said. "Dinner in 30 minutes love. I'll see you down there. Please don't be late"

The days went by and the party was tomorrow and the wedding the next. I could tell this was going to be a big-big event. I think everyone was invited.

At the party I met some very high ranking officials. I didn't know if I said the right thing or not. Phillip told me not worry about it they all know I'm a foreigner. Ok I thought does that mean they will all think I'm stupid or something? I would call myself intelligent---well in a few subjects but Phillips customs no I guess I was pretty ignorant. I need to get a book I don't want to appear stupid.

CHAPTER 31

AS THE PARTY and wedding drew closer I was getting nervous. I hadn't had any trouble finding things to do during the day. I had kept myself busy and the days went by ever so fast. There were caterers the day before the party everyone was rushing around doing what they had to do. The garden looked beautiful with flowers all over and a fountain that had coloring in it.

The day of the party that was to last almost all day long, turned out to be hectic. I rose early and got ready--- had breakfast and headed out to the courtyard to meet everyone. All day long there was, toast after toast. I don't know how everyone kept their cool and didn't get drunk. It was an adventure for sure. As evening drew close Phillip pulled me aside and said he had something for me to wear to the wedding. He pulled out a large box and opened it.

"OMG, OMG, OMG" it was a stunning necklace of diamonds *"I mean huge diamonds"* bigger than I had ever seen and ruby's. "OMG" That's all I could say. My eyes filled with tears and I started to cry.

"What's the matter Amy---don't you like it?"

"I looked up at him and said. "How could I not like it but it's so expensive."

"I love you and you are going to be my wife and you will get lots of earrings and necklaces like this so you need to get used to it. OK."

He was smiling because he knew I liked it a lot.

"I love it so much---I just don't know if I can get used to getting things like this."

I was in seventh heaven and I was looking forward to the wedding tomorrow. As the evening wound down and I had met everyone there I was exhausted. I needed to get to sleep so I was refreshed for the big day.

Morning came too quickly and I was nervous---very nervous. I messed around my room all morning. Phillip had sent a hair dresser and makeup woman up to put my best face on. I found myself loving the pampering. Then as they finished up Martha came up and said it was time to get dressed.

She helped me into my beautiful dress and stood back and looked at me and said. "Miss Amy you are so pretty and the dress fits you perfect. I'll get your veil."

A veil I hadn't thought of that. "Martha---who's going to help me with the Train when I walk down the aisle?"

"I am." She said as she put the veil on my head ever so gently. Oh wow as I looked in the full length mirror it was beautiful, flowing down my shoulders and onto the ground.

"Oh good---I feel more comfortable with you." I will have it all straightened out before you walk down the aisle and it will follow your every step. Just remember don't walk too fast.

"Hurry now Miss Amy we have to go." She helped me with the dress down the stairs (thank goodness they were wide stairs) and into a waiting carriage. The same one Phillip had proposed in. It was decorated up with calla lilies and greenery with netting & lace all over. The big white wheels had a bouquet in the center and greenery around the spokes so they looked like a rolling basket of flowers.

When we got to the wedding chapel it was decorated and fit for a King and Queen. People were standing outside to get a look at me (at me) and because there wasn't any room in the hall for them. I was savoring every minute. This was absolutely awesome.

I was led to the door and into the hall where I hesitated before walking down the aisle with gorgeous bouquet of yellow calla lilies. The music was playing ever so softly and everyone was waiting for the huge doors to open and for me to walk down the aisle. As the doors opened everyone stood up and their eyes were on me. I looked to the end of the aisle and saw Phillip standing looking at me with a warm loving smile. I knew he was happy with his choice. He also looked so very handsome.

I hadn't seen Ellen or Catherine or my other friends but did as I got to the front. They were seated in the front row and were smiling and giving me the thumbs up sign. It seemed to take forever to get down the aisle. My eyes were on Phillip and his eyes were on me. Everything seemed so perfect---except for the fact that I was marring Phillip instead of Sammy. For a moment I wondered what our wedding would have been like.

When I reached the alter I had to step up two steps---Martha came up to collect my bouquet. My wedding dress was so full I had a hard time turning in it. I could hardly move. Phillip didn't want any bridesmaids or groomsmen. He wanted only us there to be seen by the world. He said our wedding would hit world news. I had caught out of the corner of my eye as I was walking down the aisle so many people---the church was packed---it was a big church too. There were photographers and cameras everywhere. I was nervous so---so nervous.

As the minister read the words I was listening to, he said a lot of things that were normal for weddings and then he added his own thoughts about marriage and he had some interesting points. To my surprise I was listening very closely. He had us put our hand on the bible and pray. The ceremony was long much longer than traditional weddings I was used to. Then there was a traditional drinking of the royal wine that had been in the family for generations. (Ok I'm going to be drunk before this wedding is over.) Then the minister came to "does anyone here have any reason why this man and woman should not be joined in holy matrimony please speak now or forever hold your peace." There was a long lingering silence. I looked over at Phillip and he smiled and moved his lips to say I love you. My dear I will cherish you forever. It was so touching and sweet. It almost brought tears to my eyes---but I fought them back. I saw Phillip sweating and wished the minister would get on with it. I was beginning to get warm too. I think they had the thermostat turned up as high as it would go. Time seemed to go by so slowly as we waited for the minister to start talking again.

All of a sudden I heard a *'Yes we do.'* I was stunned as I turned slightly to my surprise I saw Sammy, Jason and Shelly standing in the doorway. They started slowly walking towards us. Not only did I see them but I saw a shadowy figure right behind them. "OMG!" I shouted when I saw her." I couldn't believe they were here but what was the shocker was I was seeing Sandy Jenson behind them---the kid's mom who had died from the accident in front of my house. Shocked---scared---stunned---wow what was happening?

I turned and looked at Phillip who was looking at me with a hurt look on his face and said. "Tell me that's not who I think it is. Please Amy--- tell me it's not them."
I couldn't say anything---for once in my life I was speechless..

The minister reached over and touched Phillips arm and asked. "Should I go on?" Phillip didn't say anything---he was as shocked as I was.

"We love you Amy Grant and the four of us are meant to be together. Shelly and Jason's aunt couldn't do the mother thing so she left. She went back to her old life. I have custody of the kids now and we all want you to come back home with us." As they were walking toward the alter I could see *Sandy was right behind them---she was looking at me holding her pinky up and saying Pinky Promise'* I could hear her as plain as day.

Sammy kept talking. "When I saw the picture of you and Phillip in the paper to be married I couldn't bear it I had to let you know how we felt." He looked at Shelly then Jason. "The kids feel the same way we all love you and you belong with us. We had a good life---I screwed up I know that now and I am so sorry---our life was interrupted for a while---but it can be the way it was---if you just take our hand and walk with us." Shelly dropped to her knees and with her hands clasp together and tears in her eye she said.

" 'Pinky Promise mommy' we will love you forever. Please come home."

Jason added "Pwease come home Mommy." I struggled to turn to Phillip and said,
"Phillip I don't know what to say, this has been an amazing ride but this is where I think I have to get off. Thank you for everything and am I'm truly sorry." I started to remove the necklace to return it---he grabbed my hand and with a tear in his eye said. "Keep it Amy---I will love you forever but I do believe you belong with them. It will remind you of me and how much I love

you. Go in peace and know I will always be here for you if you ever need me. My heart will ache for a long time and I may never get over you." I smiled and gave him a gentle kiss--- turned as fast as I could in that huge dress and ran to Sammy and hugged the kids and said, *'Pinky Promise I love you all too.'* Let's go home." I looked behind them and saw Sandy's shadow heading to the door, she turned and smiled at me and said, *'Pinky Promise'* I closed my eyes and when I opened them she was nowhere to be seen. I wondered if she was the one in the hotel trying to tell me I was with the wrong guy. I'll never know for sure.

I turned and blew a kiss to Phillip and turned to my family and said "let's go home."

I don't know what's going to happen when we get home but I do know it's a new beginning for all of us. I know I will cherish every moment we have together. We will have to take it life one day at a time, and one day at a time we will be a family forever.